Contents

Life in the Tide Pools 3

    Chapter One: Morning of the Homicide 4

    Chapter Two: Small Town Police 23

    Chapter Three: Homicide in Paradise 36

    Chapter Four: A Political Force 45

    Chapter Five: Best Friends 54

    Chapter Six: Arraignment and Enemies 69

    Chapter Seven: Out on Bail 77

    Chapter Eight: 7 months later 98

    Chapter Nine: Trial Day is Coming 120

    Chapter Ten: A Hearing 133

Introduction

What is the role of loyalty in the American family unit? Webster dictionary defines loyalty as, implies a faithfulness that is steadfast in the face of any temptation to renounce, desert, or betray.'

    This word gets thrown around today, especially by employers. They want employees to be loyal, but are they? I worked at a law firm, and the head attorney had his favorites. You would think the preferred would be the most loyal to the company. The favorite was in an accident. The head attorney not only held her job for months, but he also paid for her bills. Now, she has come back and worked for a few months. Then she quit abruptly for more money at a different firm. Now, the employee was clearly not loyal to the firm. The firm expressed loyalty to the specific employee. That was a mistake.

Now, one of the best examples of loyalty is the mafia. My opinions aside. They did have an honor system of extreme loyalty. At least in the early days. It reminds me of the term, honor among thieves. There is a mafia boss at the top tier, and all are to be loyal to the boss. Next are the 'made men.' They have rights to place orders but are still loyal to the boss. The wannabee that is not worthy of loyalty yet must get permission from a 'made man' to do anything. Permission was needed to hit a 'made man.' One could not go beyond the rules unless they wanted to be labeled a rat and a target. Many think the decline of power in the mafia world is because of the lack of loyalty. Loyalty is a powerful trait of one that can be trusted completely.

I recently had a conversation with my sister. We watch many true crimes on the streaming. I had asked if I committed a crime, would she turn me in? To my chagrin her answer was yes. I was surprised because I am the opposite. I am big on loyalty and protecting the family. It is an interesting character study to observe what siblings will do for one another. My siblings portrayed in this book are bonded due to tragedy and absence of appropriate parental figures. I wanted to explore how this bond would be evaluated if one of them was in true danger of being convicted of a serious crime. Does Piper believe Lincoln to be innocent? Does it matter to her?

I was interested in exploring the characters and their family connections. Piper is the older sibling, and she deems herself responsible for the family. Lincoln is the innocent little brother that depends on the older sibling. They have embraced their natural roles. Piper as an adult does not consider herself a victim. However, is she still just the terrified young girl with the world on her shoulders? What would happen to Lincoln without the complete trust between him and his sister?

Life in the Tide Pools

Tide pools near the ocean are created by isolated pockets of seawater developed by tides and rock formations. The organisms that settle and reside in these areas must survive a constantly changing ecosystem. Despite the challenges, these areas produce beautiful sea life like sea stars and barnacles.

The characteristic of a dangerous environment relates to the Baker siblings. They may have been destroyed by the negative elements unless they found a way to create beauty from bad circumstances.

Chapter One: Morning of the Homicide

Home of Esther Klink, 79 in Marathon Florida

Monday morning around 6am

He checked the bay window to make sure none of the nosy neighbors were walking their dog or going to the corner store. He stepped over Esther's body being careful not to leave any shoe prints. He did not intend to kill her. That is why he brought the mask so she would not recognize him. However, it had changed we she recognized him from the crew. His mask came off and his anger grew. He couldn't wait to get out of here. It smelled like an old antique shop or thrift store. He glanced over at the bedroom. It was neat with not very much furniture. This was going to be easy. He wouldn't have had to kill her if she would shut up.

He could not stand the crying. It made him cringe and think of his useless grandmother who was always sobbing. It was easy to choke her because of her small stature and weakness. He would not have thought himself capable of that kind of violence. He had thought of all the women in his life that were ungrateful. It was a total adrenaline rush.

Why should he have given her a chance? No one cared about his welfare. He worked hard in the hot sun all day. The women in his life were never grateful. He could not even have a beer at the bar before he was getting called home. Never once was a warm dinner or a cold beer presented to him before going home.

He went to the jewelry box and emptied the contents into his backpack. He had already taken the wedding ring and pearls off the body. He had to break the finger, but there was no way he was leaving that diamond behind. The funeral director would take it regardless. He checked all the drawers and there was nothing but junk and pictures. He did not care as he already had the envelope of $5,000.00. It was right where that dumb bi*** told everyone. She was going to pay for new stucco on the house, but she was old fashioned and was paying in cash. The disgusting, old woman announced it in front of the whole crew that she would have cash in an envelope. Not a clever idea when most of the crew have records. He was satisfied that there was nothing else of value in the small home. He went out the back and followed the back way to the beach. He dropped his mask and gloves in the public *bin. In hours, thousands of beach lovers will converge and use that trash can. He was in the clear.*

Small towns in the South are mysterious and often hold secrets. As someone from the North, Vito Ramone did not know what he was in for at this job. He only knew the transfer was to be the police chief in a small town in the Florida Keys. It was about as far from New York as he could get. If there was an opening in Alaska, he might have taken that journey. Everyone was friendly and he could not believe he now lived by the ocean. Vito was looking for a fresh start. He also wanted to conduct a mental survey of the town and see what specific change was needed. He assumed their biggest issue may be theft at the resorts. He was also told that the locals could be rowdy. Vito did not want to come in rough at first. He needed to win over the trust of the community. The first month was lonely and he really felt the absence of his daughter. Also, he would like to meet someone with which he could share the sunsets and wine. His past with women was shaky at best but he hoped there was a future with someone special.

For Vito, it was silly to think that a geographical location would have an influence on his relationships. He was hoping he could start over. His daughter would decide to go to school in Florida. Once she saw the ocean and experienced the weather he was hoping she would be charmed by Florida. If she chose a college on the mainland, he could see her as much as he wanted. He did not want to be one of those fathers just disappear after the separation or divorce. You do not divorce the children. Yes, he had high expectations from this new job and home.

    Vito was also hoping that a small-town atmosphere would bring quiet semi-retirement. He did not want to go through the political upheaval that goes with becoming a boss in the big apple. They had a small ceremony when he arrived with Marathon's small force and the government team. It was at one of the local restaurants. The best thing about it was the fresh seafood dinner. His team that worked out of the small squad were great. He had big shoes to fill from the old Chief that had been there for years.

    After the dinner he was getting a drink and the mayor motioned him to a chat on the deck. Alicia Travers was an energetic woman that took her politics seriously. Nick was familiar with these types of narcissistic families that wanted to use their positions to advance their family's values. He had a defense up as he did not want to get too close. Really, Alicia was going to size him up and see if he was an ally or an enemy. For if you were not a friend to the mayor's regime, you were considered an antagonist. She had a dress on that she overpaid for that looked like she was going to a debutant ball with billowed shoulders and all.

They did the typical small talk of the weather and the real estate market in Marathon. Alicia advised that she saw a big future for Marathon Key. They were excited to bring more large resorts and an exclusive yacht club. Alicia was quick to let Nick know that their plan will bring more money to the area. Also, the taxes will benefit the police and the rest of the first responders and government.

Alicia set her drink on the edge of the patio. "Nick, this area has been burning its assets and resources for years. As I am sure you have seen from your new home that the views and locations are priceless. Unfortunately, the recent years of turbulent weather and the rising property taxes from the water-based maintenance. Saltwater damage and the need for larger and stronger docks are a concern.

Nick finished his brandy and motioned for another from the server. "Mayor Travers. I am honored for the reception as the new Chief. However, it was not my intention to get involved deeply in politics here. I want to give the hotels the support they need."

Alicia smiled and excused herself. She thought she must keep an eye on this new Chief. They needed him to smile at the press and agree with their proposals. Time will tell.

Piper Campbell had a team meeting this morning. She had been at the Dolphin Dreams Resort since she was a teenager. Piper started there as a housekeeper and worked her way up to manager. As the hotel manager, it was her responsibility to make sure the guests and employees were happy. Piper had always been a natural leader and loved her work. She finished her makeup and carefully put on her uniform. She wore pleated white capris and a blue polo shirt. She straightened out her blue and white scarf, so she looked professional. She also always carried a crossover bag with the hotel name and a radio to contact the other managers. Her blonde hair was in a straight even ponytail. Piper had always taken pride in her appearance. She loved the motto of dressing for the job you want and not the job you have. She looked in the mirror to double-check and when she was satisfied that she looked perfect, she would head downstairs to the family.

    As young children, Piper and her younger brother, Lincoln were the dreaded Baker siblings. Their extended family were considered crooks and hustlers. They lived in paradise, but the trailer and their reputation were all too common. Their trailer was not a fun place to hang out. After Piper did her chores and made sure Lincoln was fed and clothed, they ran to the ocean. They would play with the sea animals that collected on the rocks that made smaller pools. The hermit crab races were their favorite past time. Their feet developed callouses from the coral and rocks. Playtime always meant blood from a cut or sunburn. Piper would treat their wounds and make sure Lincoln was safe. Nighttime was not safe in the trailer. Their parents would violently fight, and strange men and women were smoking and drinking. Piper would grab food and water to lock in their bedroom. When she got older, she would steal pizza or candy. She entertained Lincoln with stories and music. She always had the door locked and pushed the dresser in front. It was safe. At least enough for Lincoln to fall asleep. As Piper entered her teens she became an extraordinary beauty. Her grandmother's home became a dangerous place. The local men knew that Agnes would not pay attention to her grandchildren unless she needed them to do a chore. Piper eventually would find an empty room at the hotel at night and stay there with Lincoln. Her boss must have known but having been a local, he knew her plight at home.

Now, the Campbells were considered a model family in the small town of Marathon Key Florida. Their home was one of the nicest on the Waterfront. It was not the biggest home, but the landscaping was always kept up. They had a private dock. As a teenager Piper met her husband, Lachlan Campbell. At the time, Lachlan was on a construction crew to rebuild after one of the many hurricanes that effected the Keys in

Florida. Besides his Scottish auburn hair and goatee, he was physically fit and intelligent. Piper felt this man was dependable and had a good future. She did not have any trouble attracting men as she was a beauty pageant winner and at the time a reigning Ms. Florida Keys. Lachlan was struck dumb with her first smile. They dated for the two months that the crew was working in town. Lachlan proposed on the last day he was going to be in town. He was ten years older than Piper as she was only seventeen when they met. After that he moved there permanently from Miami. It was a short engagement and a small wedding. It was a classy ceremony in a park by the beach. The groom and his groomsmen wore traditional kilts. His cousin played the bagpipes as they walked off to the reception. Lachlan's mother and family came from Miami and stayed in the Keys for the weekend. Even Lachlan's father traveled from Scotland for the wedding.

 Piper had a lot of friends from school and coworkers from the hotel attending the wedding. As for family, it was a sore subject for Piper. Her grandmother was the only family that was not in prison or deceased. She raised Piper and her brother. Unfortunately, she was an awful woman, and many times was neglectful and abusive. Piper had made sure Agnes, her grandmother, had a dress and was sober for the event. It was a cause of anxiety for Piper and Lachlan was supportive. However, Piper only told him that Agnes was difficult and did not really relate all the information. Piper did not want to be the child that was abused. She wanted her husband to see her as a strong, confident woman. Piper also worried about her brother, Lincoln Baxter. They were only a few years apart in age, but Piper was like his mother or caretaker. She had often made sure he had food and clean clothes for school. She enrolled him in sports and made sure he was social with other boys his age. Piper was determined that he would live a thriving and comfortable life. Lincoln even stood as her 'man of honor' for her wedding. Agnes passed away after the wedding and Lachlan agreed to take Lincoln in as a brother. He stayed with them for a while until he moved to share a trailer with friends. Piper was against it, but he was an adult and there was not much she could do to stop it. She still stopped by there every day and made sure the young man was ok.

    Lincoln Baker was incessantly under the shadow of his older sister, Piper Campbell. She tried lovingly to shelter him from the chaos of their family. Lincoln understood more than Piper thought. He could see the deterioration of his parents and their trailer. He heard the fights and the sound of his father's fists against the skin of his mother's face. He never bonded with his mother. She was not the face he remembered putting him to sleep or giving him food. Piper was always making sure he washed and that his clothes were clean. He knew there were times when she would give her portion of food to him. She would always tell him that she ate earlier. Lincoln knew that was a lie and was feverishly loyal to his sister.

Piper- 9, Lincoln – 7

Imagine living less than a mile from the ocean. Different bright shades of blue. Piper liked to draw as a small child. It was an activity that did not cost a lot of money. Michalea was still sober at certain moments when she was holding a part time job. Piper asked for Christmas one year the large box of crayons. She wanted the different shades of blue to draw the ocean. In school, she had learned that there were nineteen different blue colors. She saw this in the ocean. At sunrise it would be sky blue, blue violet and robin's egg. During the hottest part of the day, it was light blue and turquoise. In the sunset was Piper's favorite, manatee blue water. Of course, her parents were drunk that year and there were no presents. Piper's teacher had taught her how to mix colors to make what she wanted. That was Piper's best life lesson from the one person around her that genuinely cared. Piper took that lesson throughout her life. She did not start out with the basic things she needed in life. Piper had to use what she could get and make it into what she wanted.

Piper headed to the kitchen after she stopped to throw some laundry into the dryer. She straightened up the laundry room and started the washer as well. They had a housekeeper, Anna, which was there but Piper was not afraid to get her hands dirty. She never forgot her roots as a lower-class kid roaming the beaches in the Keys. Once in the kitchen she would examine the children and make sure that they looked presentable for school. Rory was the first born. He was eleven years old now. He had the brawn, height, and muscles of his father. His wavy blonde hair was a replica of his pretty mother. Rory was the 'apple of his mother's eye.' Their personalities complemented each other. His room was always neat and his hair and appearance as close to perfect as possible. He was the kind of kid that turned in his work early and sat in front of the class. Isla was their daughter and their middle child. She was a tall gangly child of nine. Isla was the fiery red head of the family and had bounds of childhood energy. She was an athlete as she played volleyball and soccer. Her room tended to be messy. She was a daddy's girl, and Lachlan always took her to and witnessed her games. Fiona was a family baby at five years old. She spent the most time with her nanny, Charlotte. She had short blond hair and never met a stranger. Her favorite was her uncle, Lincoln.

    Lincoln always made fun of Piper because her housekeeper and nanny were both older women. He said that Piper refused to have someone younger or prettier around her handsome husband. Piper disagreed and said that it was because they are wiser and more experienced. Secretly, a small part of her was glad that they would not be a temptation for her husband. She had seen that while watching Lifetime and did not want to take a chance. However, she would never admit that to Lincoln. Piper appeared cold or irreverent to most people. She had overcompensated all her life. Lincoln and Piper were poor kids in school. All she could do as a young girl was to make sure their persons were presentable. Piper could never drop her façade unless it was just her and Lincoln. She felt vulnerable to anyone else.

Piper came into the kitchen and Lincoln was sitting at the breakfast table. This was odd because he was never at their house this early. She noticed that his hair was a mess, and he was dressed too warmly for the weather. There was also a dirty blue backpack on the table. Piper greeted her husband by the counter as he read the paper. She gave him a warm kiss and his lunchbox for the day. Lachlan owned the construction company now. A lot of it had to do with Piper working overtime and getting promoted at the hotel. Lachlan was also a prime candidate to run for the mayoral spot in the Marathon Key. His only viable opponent was Alicia Travers who was the sitting Mayor. There was no love lost between the two candidates' families.

Lachlan was a 'gentle giant' and appreciated the drive his wife had to run their family and finances. He knew the first time he saw her at the hotel. They had come to clean up and do construction after a particularly bad hurricane. He was fascinated but the young woman that controlled all aspects of the hotel simultaneously. He traveled a lot for work, so he had not had too many long-term relationships. Once he met Piper, he wanted to settle down. She wanted to stay in the Florida Keys. Lachlan agreed and with family help and Piper having good savings. He excelled in the company and soon bought out the company and based administration in Florida with Piper. They were now a power couple. Their most stringent competition was with The Travers family. Lachlan was not keen on being a mayoral candidate, but Piper had insisted. He agreed that it would be a great opportunity for the children's future.

  Piper checked Rory and Isla to make sure they were presentable and finished their breakfast. Fiona would already be out with Charlotte. She had breakfast at school and then she had a swimming class. She finished the lunches for the children and made sure they knew what they had scheduled that day. Piper had all sorts of boards and schedules in the house. Lachlan then took the other two children to school. Piper had Anna go ahead and start on the bedrooms. She then sat at the table by Lincoln.

  "Ok, Linc what are you doing here this early? Did you lose your job again? Did a chick rob you and leave you on the road? I cannot wait to hear this."

Piper tried to straighten his hair, but he motioned her away.

"Nothing is wrong Sis; I just need a ride to work." He continued eating his eggs.

"Where is your car, did you get in an accident again? I told you about hanging out with those losers at Oyster's Bar." Piper took his plate and threw it into the sink.

"No, it's at home. I just had to see a guy around here this morning and I need a ride if I'm going to make it to work on time. Piper stared at him for a while.

"Ok, I will give you a ride if you get that nasty backpack off my table." Lincoln smiled and hugged Piper. It was nice as he rarely lets her in anymore. She hoped he was ok. Lincoln grabbed his backpack and went to wait in the Jeep.

Piper climbed in the Jeep with Lincoln and headed to Hog Key. Their crew was repairing docks in that area. Lincoln was playing with his phone. "Sis, why can't I just get a job with Lachlan doing construction?"

"Linc, I told you it would look like favoritism. Besides, I want you to stand up on your own two feet. We are better than our no-good parents."

Lincoln said, "Is it because your rich husband does not want his loser brother-in-law around? Just another no-good Baxter from the swamp?"

Piper was shocked, "No way, Lachlan loves you like his own child. We decided you had to make your own path. You are a man now; Lincoln and it is about time you took responsibility. I know your boss would love you to go above and beyond. That diving school was not cheap, and neither were your certification fees. Why don't you ask for more work?"

She pulled up to the worksite and turned to Lincoln. "Sweetie, I promise if you work hard, it will pay off. You will even introduce me to that girlfriend I know you are hiding?"

Lincoln rolled his eyes and jumped from the Jeep. Piper stopped him. "Wait, here is a few hundred. Get a haircut and new backpack and take the mystery girl on a nice date to a real restaurant, not the bar. Oh, and I am the rich one, not Lachlan. Don't get it twisted, little brother." Piper winked at him, and he smiled. She watched her brother walk in and checked her phone. She felt like he had something more to say. She was going to be late. She made a mental note to take him to dinner sometime this week.

Piper knew who he was seeing. She just wanted him to admit that he was still seeing Payton. Payton grew up with them and was Piper's best friend for a while. That was until Lincoln hit puberty and became obsessed with Payton. She caused both a lot of heartache and legal bills. She loved Payton as family, but she wanted more for Lincoln. Payton's family was wealthy and would never allow Lincoln and Payton to marry.

Lincoln walked to the crew and started to put on his dive gear. Jacob and Elias came over to the equipment truck. Jacob grabbed a donut and coffee. "Hey Lincoln, you are on time. Did you get grounded last night? Do you think Piper would leave that Viking and come live with me?"

Lincoln usually tried to ignore them, but he was not in the mood. "Jacob, have you seen your ex-girlfriends? The zoo had to round them up after you were done dating." Elias laughed and poured his coffee out.

"Damn, that stuff will rot your gut. We had better stop going to Oyster's on Sunday nights. Lincoln, what happened to you last night? Did you get lucky? You know I need you as my wingman. Jacob scares them away with his chest hair."

Lincoln replied: "I was there for a while. What did you get kicked out again? You must stop drinking so much, Elias. However, you are right about Jacob."

Jacob punched Elias in the arm. The boss yelled at the men to get going. They had a stucco job in town after this work. It has been slow lately and they need work. Lincoln ignored them and went to the water. He just wanted his hangover to go away.

Payton had taught Lincoln to dive so he could get his scuba license. They took any excuse to be alone. Lincoln had asked Payton to marry him dozens of times. In this western society it is not the norm anymore for the parents to have to approve of a marriage. However, Payton's large family was from old wealth in the South. They had migrated to the Florida Keys from Savannah Georgia. Payton was expected to marry well. That meant with a wealthy family that had a good reputation. These values were instilled in her and her siblings throughout their youth. Payton had reveled in being with the Baker siblings as youth for an escape. She found Piper to be like a wild cheetah, strong and intelligent. She was a breathtaking beauty. Piper was a born leader and never showed a hint of weakness. Payton was the opposite. She was emotional and delicate. Her beauty worked against her and made her a victim. She did not like confrontation in the family. She loved being a police officer because she was in charge. Once the uniform was put on, she was respected and her opinion mattered. Lincoln was capricious and wild. He was fiery and devoted to his older sister. Payton also fiercely mesmerized him. He was attracted to her humor and delicate sensibilities. Lincoln had never shown interest in any other local.

As in any good love story, there is an obstacle for love by an external antagonist. Piper was not a fan of the relationship between her brother and Payton. She was worldly and knew that the poor kid in town did not end up with the debutante. Her motive to separate the couple is pure and protective. She loves them both and wants no harm if it isn't necessary. A formidable opponent for Lincoln's pursuit of Payton is her family. They accepted Lincoln as a needy figure in the town. However, he was only a figurehead of their charity. He would never be accepted as a spouse for their daughter.

Lincoln had made a formal attempt to get Payton's hand in marriage when they were in their mid-twenties. Piper had two children at the time and was not as diligent in watching Lincoln. Lincoln had bought a dapper blue suit and shaved and cut his blond locks. He looked as handsome as ever. He went to the Fisher household and had a meeting with Payton's parents. He outlined his desire to open a diving business for boat charters. He also vowed to protect Payton and make sure she was happy and secure. The parents informed him that they would consider the offer. Lincoln felt good until he heard that the Fishers were telling everyone at the boat club and mocking Lincoln. In their world, he was from a bad family and had no future worthy of their daughter. Not even a week later, Payton's parents had organized a date between Payton and Declan Travers. The athlete son of the current mayor, Alicia Travers. Lincoln was furious because it was a blatant refusal of his worthiness to be in their family.

Lincoln was known for his spontaneous decisions. When it came to the locals, the Keys is a small town. Eventually, Lincoln ran into Declan in a bar. Declan was with friends and began to verbally harass Lincoln. It finally came to a boiling point, and the bar tender asked them all to leave. Once outside, Lincoln was outnumbered. Declan's friends were all athletic and trained. However, Lincoln had learned a long time ago how to defend himself. Piper and he had more than once found themselves confronted by bad circumstances in the town. Unfortunately, Declan had visible injuries when the police showed up. Lincoln was arrested and it was important in the gossip circles. Piper of course provided a good lawyer for her brother. She also was able to coordinate a good conclusion to the case by catering to the Travers family. Lincoln had promised Piper that he would not see Payton in a romantic relationship after that night.

Chapter Two: Small Town Police

The Marathon Key Florida police building was a substation. The emergency 911 service and fire department went through Monroe County Sheriff's Office. The paramedics were part of a private company and roamed up and down the keys. The coroner was with the Monroe County Medical Examiner. This was a part of the Sheriff's Office. The police were limited and in a small pink building on the main road. They had two patrol officers and a detective. The Chief has just retired. It was difficult to get someone qualified that would be willing to take a job in a remote area of the Florida Keys. It is a beautiful ocean setting; however, good housing is expensive, and the weather can be terrifying in the hurricane season.

    The new Chief was from New York and was trying to fit in as much as possible. Vito Ramone had been in town for a month trying to assimilate to the small station. They mostly dealt with petty thefts and tossing drunks into the sober tank. However, they also did cover crimes to do with the hotels and marinas. So, this would include rampant prostitution, assaults, and drug busts. Vito was a big guy with a commanding presence. He would get ribbing from the locals for his accent. He had an olive complexion that agreed with the sun. His dark hair was cut low, and he was always dressed well. He was a good-looking guy and liked his freedom. He was divorced and had a teenage daughter back in New York. He was looking forward to his daughter spending her first summer with him in Florida. It was a rumor that he was a flirt. The story was about an affair with a detective's wife and was forced to transfer to Florida. Vito was a good sport and never denied the allegations. He always thought it made him more interesting. Really, he had spent years on a difficult case. After that he wanted a break from the big city crime. He also had a falling out with his ex-wife and needed a fresh start.

    Vito had met his ex when they were both new beat officers in Brooklyn. Jenny was blonde and tough. She was tiny but passed all the training tests at the top of the class. Vito was attracted to her spunk. It had taken a few months, but she had finally agreed to go out for a drink after their shift. Once she let her tough exterior down, she found that he was handsome and smart. They had a quick engagement as Jenny found out she was pregnant with their daughter. They had a huge wedding with the police formal uniforms and an Italian buffet. Jenny decided to stay at home after the baby. Vito felt that she resented him for that. However, he made sure it was her decision. Their relationship had not been the same since their daughter was born. They fell into a pattern and were comfortable with each other. They also wanted their girl to grow up in a stable two parent household. Vito enjoyed being a father and made sure he took care of his family.

Years passed and he was promoted to detective. He caught a case of a young couple from the Bushwick area of Brooklyn. The victim was an artist named Conrad Magnusson. He lived in a loft above his gallery. His longtime girlfriend, Vivienne Simon, was a French national that had been in the country since she was a child. They had responded to a 911 call from a domestic. Vito was wary of all domestic situations because you never know the level of threat. It might be an extremely dangerous scene or just a squabbling couple or roommates.

The patrol officers called in the detectives as they had a deceased male, 36, partially clothed and with a visible injury to the head. They had located the live-in girlfriend, Vivienne, hiding in a closet with a fire poker. She had called the police on her cell phone complaining that she had been beaten. It is presented as a case of self-defense. The police officer separated the girlfriend in the bedroom, closed the scene, and called the detectives. Vito examined the deceased as the medical examiner was taking their evidence. He had an obvious deformity of the forehead. He was bare chested with only jeans on. Several paintings were damaged, and the loft area appeared to be where the event occurred. He had long brown hairs in his hand and bloody knuckles.

Vito went to speak with the suspect. He entered the bedroom, and she was seated on the bed in a lace top and khaki shorts. Her white shirt was covered in blood. She had numerous facial injuries and abrasions. She was petite and only a little over five feet. Vito thought she looked helpless and small on the large California king bed with a giant elaborate headboard. He noticed that everything in the apartment was garish and oversized. She was shaking and he asked her a few questions. She could barely get her name out. Vito let the medics attend her and had her escorted to the station after the hospital.

Vito had become obsessed with the case. The man was a well-known painter in the city. The young woman was villainized in the press and by his family. It had been declared self defense by the police and the coroner. His family made a lot of noise and continued to harass the girlfriend. Vito had helped her move out of the loft and they spent intimate time together. Eventually, he had to choose between Vivienne or his family. She took a flight to France one way and Vito went home to Brooklyn. Vito never forgave himself for letting her leave. Especially since his wife left him soon after. He wanted to try something different and when the transfer opportunity to Florida came up, he readily accepted.

There was one detective that managed the investigations. It was Serenity Jackson. She was a no-nonsense woman who took her work very seriously. She believed that small-town crimes are just as important as in larger areas. She wanted to make Marathon the safest city in Florida. She was married to the fire chief, Louis Jackson. The rest of the fire department were volunteers. They had a son that was a first-year student in Florida State.

Detective Serenity Jackson sat in the morning briefing. This was her first day back after her leave. Her last Chief was Carl Cooper, and he had retired. She was so devastated that they joked she was grieving. Carl had been with the substation for 20 years. He was now living it up in Orlando with his wife and daughter. Vito was trying to win the respect and loyalty of Serenity. He was supportive of the fact that she had been collaborating with the previous chief for years. However, Vito intended to make some changes and make the position his own. He hoped she would adjust well. If not, he would have to discuss their choices. The others in the morning briefing were two patrolmen.

Clifton Graser was a local in Marathon. He was young and went to the academy in Manatee County Florida. He had longer brown hair with some curls on the end. He was a smaller guy but could handle himself in a fight. He still hung out with the locals, and they respected him when he was in uniform. Payton Fisher was the other full time patrol officer. She was an animated personality in her early thirties. Payton was also the best friend of Piper Campbell. They had known each other their whole lives. Payton was the fifth child of a large close family. Piper and Lincoln often spent time at their house when they were younger. It was like a haven for them. Lincoln had once called Payton's mother 'mummy' which he was told was a Scottish/Gaelic term for mother. Payton was a sexy brunette with dimples and large hazel eyes. She practiced karate and was an avid runner and diver. She helped Lincoln practice and get his diving license.

    Chief Vito started the meeting with general information. They had one squad car and a suburban. He assigned Payton the squad car. He decided to ride with Serenity in the SUV so they can be seen out in the community. Stella was the office manager and receptionist. She kept the small station running. She was in her fifties and lived in a small condominium on Big Pine Key. Clifton was to take the bicycle to travel around the large resorts. The larger resorts often had security, but they wanted to make sure the tourists felt safe. They make their money off the deep see fishing and the hotels. The chief concluded the morning meeting, and they grabbed the muffins brought in by Stella.

Payton sat on the edge of Clifton's desk. "So, you are on nerd patrol today. What did you do to piss off the new chief?" She ruffled his hair.

"Knock it off Payton. You know I damaged the patrol car last week. It was not even a big deal. I swerved to avoid a turtle in the road."

Payton laughed and leaned closer to Clifton. She liked to make him nervous. "Was it a female turtle? Maybe wearing a neon pink bikini?"

Stella interrupted. "Clifton one of the resorts has a car being towed and needs a report for the tow guy, you want to handle that?"

Clifton motioned Payton to leave him alone. "I would love to be of service somewhere else." Clifton grabbed his gloves and helmet and left.

Vito came out of his office. "Payton, don't you have a city you need to patrol?"

Payton grabbed her hat and water. "Sorry chief, heading out now. I'll be out on speed patrol." She watched him go back to his office. Serenity was working on her computer. Payton passed the desk. "He is seriously hot. I saw him at the marina the other day and it was all abs."

Serenity laughed. "You know Payton, you are too much. You really need to get married."

"Why, it's so much fun to be single in this town. Tourists never stay more than a week. That is the perfect length for me." See you later." Payton waved to Stella and left.

Piper pulled into her reserved spot at the Dolphin Dreams Resort. The owner lived on a private island off Key West. He trusted the oceanfront property in the hands of the managers. Piper was the general manager and managed guests, front desk, and housekeeping. There was also a marina manager. Jason Nestle oversaw anything to do with the watersports or boating expeditions for the guests. Piper kept her distance from Jason. He had been in some trouble when they were kids, and she did not trust him. However, he was an expert when it came to fishing and watersports. Piper knew he was the best man for the job. The night manager oversaw the bar and handled any guest's needs after the day staff leave. Inez Engers was the ultimate night owl. She arranged specials and theme nights for the bar. Their bar was immensely popular with tourists. Piper knew she needed all these people to make the hotel run seamlessly. Piper had her eye on buying out the owner eventually. He was less interested in the resort these days. She had been saving their money and waiting for the right time to present a business plan to the owner.

She had Lachlan working his crew overtime in the tourist season.

She was determined to change the reputation of her family name, Baker. Mostly so Lincoln would have a prosperous life. Lincoln did not know that his sister had trust for him to receive when he was thirty. She did not feel he was ready yet. She wanted him to get his own diving boat and marry soon. She had hints that he was seeing somebody. He had not introduced her to Piper, so she knew it was someone he was embarrassed about. She just hoped her instincts were wrong and it was not Payton. Lincoln always valued the opinion of his older sister.

Both their parents were in prison by the time Piper was ten years old. Mikaela and Thomas Baker were drug users and that was what they had in common. They lived in a trailer at the back of Mikaela's mother's house. Agnes and Tom did not get along. Once Mikaela had Piper, Agnes became bitter and did not want anything to do with Tom's children. The trailer was small, hot, and crowded. Their parents spent a lot of time in the local bars. Mikaela did manage a small job as a housekeeper at the Flamingo Inn part time. It was enough to get food and keep the electricity on. They got home late and would often pass out. Piper kept the trailer clean and made sure Lincoln always had breakfast. If they were out of food, she would steal from Agnes. It was dangerous because if she were caught, Agnes would rack her knuckles with a wooden spoon. After breakfast, Piper and Lincoln would go around the hotels and collect cans for recycling. This would give them enough to go to the laundromat. Piper knew the locals looked down on them. She made sure they were always clean and presentable. In the afternoons, they would wander around the beaches. They would collect rocks and make souvenirs to sell to the tourists. The hotel workers were constantly chasing them away. They did not care as that money meant they would eat that night. Piper would hide the money under Agnes' house in a jar. She knew if her parents saw it, the money would be used for drugs or beer. At least with their parents, Piper had free reign to mother Lincoln and worked for their money.

    One day Piper and Lincoln returned from school. The trailer was destroyed. The windows and doors were broken. Every piece of furniture was out on the lawn. The police had raided the trailer and found a stash of meth. Both parents were arrested and eventually sentenced to ten years each. There was a woman there with the police who said she was there to take the children. She grabbed Lincoln first and he screamed and fought. He had never been without Piper. Piper knew they only had one choice if they were not to be separated. She ran to Grandma Agnes. She bargained with her grandmother. She was a ten-year-old that was wise beyond her years.

Piper went through the back door and found Agnes sitting at the kitchen table smoking and working on a puzzle. Piper sat down and asked for permission to speak. She knew that Agnes appreciated formality. Agnes also liked to be the center of attention and felt that she was in charge. Agnes told her she had five minutes because her show was coming on.

"Agnes, I researched it at the library in case something like this happened. You will be considered the foster parent of Lincoln and I both. That means you get two checks from the state. Also, you are then eligible for Medicaid and food stamps. We will sleep in the attic and make that our domain. I will take care of all of Lincoln's needs, and you can have his money straight out. I will clean the house and take care of the yard. In exchange, I will get half my check. You can still be mostly child free and have enough to pay your rent and go to bingo. We will never talk back, and I will handle the school, so they don't bother you."

Agnes took a long look at Piper. This ten-year-old with long blond braids and dressed in an old but neat dress. She was amused. Agnes was surprised that she felt pride in this small child. This was her granddaughter, and she had a chance to be something. Agnes would take them in, but she would have to prepare this child for the real world. Agnes would show no mercy and never give any affection to these children. She would protect them as no one would mess with a Baxter if she were alive.

Agnes put out her cigarette and slipped on her sandals. She motioned for Piper to get out of the way. She checked her makeup in the mirror and walked out the back door. Piper ran after her and silently prayed she would show them mercy. The older woman went over to the case worker and police officer. Lincoln was in the back seat of the woman's car sobbing. The case worker saw her approaching and held out her hand to introduce herself. Agnes ignored her and went right up to the officer. She then calmly said, "Jimmy, I changed your diapers, and I know everyone in this town. If you do not get my grandson out of that stranger's car, I will let your lovely wife know why you always patrol at the hourly rate motels on night shift. I'm sure the manager there wondered why you took the women into the same room for their "punishments." Do I make myself clear or do we start making calls?"

The officer turned and picked up Lincoln. He placed him next to Piper and walked away. The case worker ran after him, and they stood arguing for a while. After that Piper and Lincoln were fostered by Agnes. They did not have the love of parents, but they had a safe place to sleep.

Piper went to her office and checked the availability for the night. They were full and had no vacancies. That was impressive for a Monday night. She worked on the schedule and returned emails and calls. She had a text from Lachlan. He wanted her to pick up Chinese for dinner that night. It used to be that he would send "sexy" texts to her during the day. Piper made sure she kept up her looks. Her hair was done at least once a week, and she went to the gym every other day. She was constantly flirted with by the male hotel guests. Some were rich businesspeople with tans and style. Now, with the children and work they have turned into every other boring married couple. She was not complaining as she loved Lachlan and knew she was lucky. They could grab a weekend away in Miami soon, just the two of them. Lincoln could watch the older two and they could leave the baby with the nanny. She made a mental note to speak with Lachlan tonight.

She picked up a picture from her desk. It was her and Lincoln as children posing in the marina. They were young and tanned with dumb smiles. They never had anything material but were always together. She smiled at his silly grin. Her own children would never feel the neglect that they had. Piper worked hard to make sure the next generation was set up for success. Her fear was always that addiction would affect Lincoln. Almost like a virus that would infect him.

Chapter Three: Homicide in Paradise

Monroe County Sheriff's Department 911 Center Call, Noon on Monday

Operator: Monroe County 911, Do you need police, fire, or ambulance?

Caller: I am not sure. She is dead. We need the police. Oh my god, Esther!

Operator: Ok, mam'n, is there a pulse? Can you do CPR?

Caller: No, her neck is all bruised and twisted. She's not breathing. She's so cold, please come soon!

Operator: Ok, what is the address?

Caller: 104 Seashell Drive, please hurry.

The dispatcher contacted the substation to say that they had a body. Stella answered and asked them for the information again. They did not get that many bodies. She went to Vito's office, and he was working on the budget. "Chief, we have a body over on Seashell, residence of Esther Klink."

"Ok, Stella, go ahead and call the county for the coroner to be on call. I will radio Payton to start over there. Serenity, you may go as well. We do not know what we have yet. If it is natural, we may get away by just contacting the funeral director. Let me know what you have."

Payton had just given a speeding ticket to a tourist. They think they can drive at whatever speed they want because it is one road. She was now parked at the marina having just finished her break. Her radio went off, *"Payton, we have a body at 104 Seashell, need you to go check it out and secure the scene. Serenity will meet you there. Over."* "10-4."

Payton hit the lights and turned out of the parking lot. She had not been on a body scene in a long time. Usually, it just turns out to be a heart attack or stroke victim. They did have a consistent number of elderly residents, especially in the winter months. Payton turned down the street and immediately noticed the woman in the street waving her arms. Payton parked in front and put on gloves. She activated the body camera. She motioned for the woman to wait on the sidewalk. Payton looked around and everything looked normal on the outside. She walked up the front steps, and the door showed no damage. It was ajar so she would have to check with the neighbor to see if they entered this way. She entered the home carefully so as not to disturb any evidence. She saw the victim as she turned into the living room. She was wearing her robe, and her head was in the hallway. She was deceased. Payton did not bother with pulse as she was already deformed on the neck. Her skin was cold and stiff. The purple color of lividity was already appearing. The victim had been dead for hours. She radioed into Stella that this looked like a homicide. She backed out of the house and retrieved the crime scene tape. She placed it over the front stairs and the yard. Payton then approached what she assumed was a neighbor.

"Ok, Miss Golden, I have the name associated with this property as an Esther Klink, is that correct?" Payton wrote down the woman's information from her license as if she might be a witness.

"Yes, oh, I'm sorry, this is just so awful. She was supposed to come over for lunch. The stucco on her house was being redone. She did not want to be there and deal with all the noise. Well, I came over to get her and there was no answer. We have each other's keys, so I opened it and she……. her neck, oh my god, who would do this?"

"Can you tell me does she live here with anybody?" Payton tried to get her report completed and then she would hand over the scene to Serenity as the investigator.

"No, Esther did not have any close family. She stays down here all year round. She is active at the senior center. She had money from her late husband. I can't imagine anyone would think she was rich. She was normally very frugal. The construction guy talked her into the stucco work."

Payton saw Serenity pulling up in the SUV. "Thank you, Miss Golden. Go ahead and wait at your house. I will give the detective your information."

Serenity jumped out as she was putting on gloves. "Hey Payton, what do we have here?"

"Elderly female, deceased, possible broken neck, and other smaller injuries. No forced entry. No known next of kin. I will have Stella see if she can find a relative." Payton grabbed her radio.

Serenity put on footies and entered the home. The old woman did not put up much of a fight. She must have been caught by surprise. There was no forced entry, so Serenity was betting that she knew the intruder. These women did not just open their doors to anybody. There was ransacking in the kitchen and especially the bedroom. Serenity did not see a jewelry box, but the picture of Esther showed a lot of jewelry. Serenity radioed Stella to give notice to the nearby pawn shops to look out for a man with women's jewelry. From the look of the neck, this was a strong young man. One that was not fond of older ladies or women. Serenity hoped that they did not have a killer out there targeting elderly women. In a state like Florida, which would cause a mass panic. The older citizens often moved to Florida to get away from crime and severe weather.

Outside, Payton was on the radio with Stella when a work truck pulled up. It was Marina Construction, owned by Ignacio Menendez. Jacob and Elias jumped out of the cab of the truck. Payton saw Lincoln sitting in the passenger seat. He looked awful and would not look in her direction. Serenity came out and told Payton to get the county forensics out here. They had a homicide here. Serenity then went to Ignacio.

"How you guys doing? This is a crime scene now. What is your business?" Serenity looked in the bed of the truck at Lincoln and then in the cab.

Ignacio lit a cigarette. "We were scheduled to redo the stucco today for Ms. Klink. He reached into the truck. "Here is the work order. She was to pay $5000, and we were to get it completed in 2 days. What happened, did she get into it with her old man or something?"

Serenity took the paper and handed it to Payton. "This is evidence now. Ms. Klink is dead, and you are all going to need to make statements. I would appreciate if you would follow the Officer here to the substation."

Ignacio put out his smoke. "Sorry, Serenity, that is awful. I had no idea. We were just here yesterday to do the estimate. Yea, Jacob and Elias, get back in."

Payton pulled out with the following pickup. She looked in the rearview and Lincoln still looked solemn. They pulled into the substation. She had them all go in and have a seat in the small waiting area. Vito came out and Clifton was back. Vito addressed the group.

"Gentleman, we have a homicide non-natural death in our small town. This is not New York, and I don't do well with little old ladies being snuffed out for money. You will all be questioned one by one as soon as Serenity returns from the scene. In the interim you are not allowed to speak to one another at all. If I hear a conversation, I will put you into a cell. Now the a/c in the jail section is on the fritz, so believe me you want to stay out here. Do we all understand? Do not ask the officers when you are going home. If you must use the facilities, you can raise your hand, and your phone will remain with the officer. If I see you on your phones, I will take them, and it will take five weeks of court to get it back. We will provide water and food as needed. Now, if you think you are cute and want to flirt with Officer Payton here. I give her permission to use non-lethal force. You got me?"

All the men nodded. Jacob advised that his partner and him have a newborn. He wanted to at least let her know where he was in case of an emergency. Vito thought for a minute. He agreed to have Stella contact his home. They all had children of various ages and understood his concern.

Vito had a commanding presence, and few wanted to go toe to toe with him. This was his first homicide in Marathon, and he wanted everything to go by the book. He felt confident leaving Payton with the witnesses. Clifton was sent to take a statement from the neighbor that found the body. Vito went back to his office with Stella to get everything organized.

"Ok, Stella. The coroner and forensics from the County are on the way to the house. When Serenity is done, I want her back here to take the witness statements with me. Clifton needs to stay at the crime scene until the body is moved. We are a small department, but homicide is the largest crime. We need to stay organized, and everything must be documented. Until we notify the next of kin, I don't want anyone outside of here or the Sheriff to know anything. Not only will we look incompetent, but we may end up with terrified senior citizens. We don't want to alert anyone until we have more information."

Payton was at the front desk typing her report and watching the witnesses. She tried not to stare at Lincoln. She looked back and Vito was talking on his phone. Stella was in the same room on the radio. Payton was not sure she could get a message to Lincoln. This was not a good situation. She wanted to alert Piper that her brother was here. However, it was not appropriate in her position to do that. She also wanted to speak to Lincoln and tell him not to say anything without a lawyer. She knew for sure that it would violate her virtue as an officer. Her phone buzzed and it was a text from her fiancée. Of course, wedding stuff. Payton had a wedding the next year to Declan Travers. He was a professional soccer player and now is the Mayor of Monroe County's son. They made a stunning couple. Declan had tried to get Payton to leave the department, but she loved the work. She sent him a text that there was a big case, and she would contact him later. Piper and Lincoln were Payton's life when they were growing up. Especially, when they were with Agnes, Payton's house was a haven. Now, she was staring at Lincoln, and something was not right. She tried to concentrate on the report. All she wanted to do was hug Lincoln and make it better. He always had these sad eyes.

    She could not believe they had been lovers for so long now. They tried desperately to get married or run away. Their families always got in the way. She could feel his frustration from her seat. They had always had a connection and were able to know when the other felt a strong emotion. Why was he nervous about the death of a random local? Lincoln would attract danger and trouble like a cat to the saucer. Payton knew he was gentle and emotional. They all had been through so much not too long ago after the confrontation with Declan. Payton's engagement to Declan had satisfied her parents for a while. Now, they were pushing for it and wanted the arrangements completed. Lincoln and she had been having arguments about what to do about the looming wedding. Now, he was being questioned about a random death.

Serenity was waiting outside the house as the forensics team from Monroe County documented the scene. This was unusual in this town. There were already nosy neighbors lining the street. She was glad that Clifton arrived when he did as this was a homicide scene. The coroner was on the way to get the body as an autopsy needed to be done. It looked like whomever the intruder was knew what they were looking for at the house. This was not a lavish neighborhood that usually was targeted for robbery. Also, Serenity thought Mrs. Klink must have known the killer. Why else kill the victim. She was not only elderly, but frail and could not put up a fight. The victim had a small social circle. So, the killer knew that she was having the house construction done. Why would they pick that morning when it was inevitable that the body would be discovered the same day? Why not do it on any other day when she would not have visitors? The workers would have to be questioned thoroughly. Right now, they are persons of interest.

Chapter Four: A Political Force

Alicia Travers was in her office overlooking the ocean. She was born and raised in the Florida Keys. She started out in real estate under the name of Alicia Wilcox. She was successful and married and merged with a fellow realtor called Bryan Travers. It was an extravagant wedding on the ocean. Everything that Alicia did was large and glamorous. She ran unopposed to the mayor's position. They had one child, Declan Travers. He was a star soccer player in the U.S. and went to two Olympics representing America. She was meeting with her chief of staff, Walter, and her husband joined them in the office. There was a call from Marathon Key that a homicide had occurred in the neighborhood involving an elderly woman. Walter took the call and thought the mayor may want to address the incident for the locals.

"Madame Mayor, we have an elderly female killed in her home on Marathon key. No suspects yet. The coroner is on the way now to remove the body for autopsy. They do have witnesses at the substation. I think it would be good if you went on the news tonight with the Sheriff and addressed the locals. We don't want a panic that there is someone going around killing old ladies."

Bryan interrupted. "This may be just what we need to get you back in the spotlight. Payton is at the substation. If they can get this solved quickly it will be a good news story. Then, we announce the wedding date between our son and the police officer that helped solve the murder. This is perfect. I mean it is a tragedy, but we cannot bring her back. Walter, see if this murder victim has any next of kin. No matter how distant of a relative I want their face on tv."

Alicia thought for a moment. "Ok, I like it. Schedule a press conference at the County building asap for the morning. Contact the new Chief and let him know that we need some kind of statement by the morning. We don't have much time so let's get moving. I want Declan and Payton there as well."

Bryan stood and joined his wife by the window. "Now we can see whose side the Chief is on, dear. This will be his first time in the political spotlight."

She smiled. "If he is smart, he will work with us and the sheriff to get this solved and out of the news. On the other hand, if it turns out to be a local, we can use that to get rid of him. Just think, the new chief settled in and the first murder in years follows. No one will feel safe. Especially, the elderly snowbirds and tourists. We can get someone in there that can really get something done. I have a nephew who is a patrol officer in Orlando. This may be the best time to promote the boy."

Back at the substation Chief Vito was expecting Serenity back soon. The forensics were done but it was a clean scene. The intruder wore gloves and was careful about shoes. There may have been something under her nails or on the broken finger so that it was sent to the lab in Miami. They asked for a rush but there was no guarantee. It looked like this may be a circumstantial case. Vito was meeting with Stella and getting their one interrogation room ready. Vito took the call from the mayor's office. He also spoke with the Monroe County Sheriff. Now, they wanted a press conference in the morning. They needed some kind of information. They were losing time getting something together. So far, they only knew what had happened. The why and the who were the parts that needed solving. Serenity should be back soon. They would split the witnesses to make the interviews go quicker. The mayor agreed to do what she can to push the forensics through the red tape. It was going to be a long afternoon and night for all.

Serenity returned to the station. Clifton was at the scene securing the location. The men were getting anxious in the waiting area. Payton watched as

Serenity went to Vito's office. She had to be careful, but she needed to warn Lincoln to stay quiet. He was impetuous even as a child and she knew he may lose his temper.

Serenity grabbed coffee and brought Ignacio back to the interview room. Vito grabbed Jacob into his office. That left Elias and Lincoln. Stella had gone to get pizza for dinner. This was Payton's chance to speak to Lincoln.

Serenity sat down with Ignacio. She explained first that they are just being detained as witnesses. They had direct contact with the victim yesterday and today.

"Ignacio, we appreciate your cooperation. Now, you were scheduled to fix the stucco on the victim's house, correct?"

"Yes, I did an estimate with her just yesterday. I had to bring the crew because we had another job right after. We looked at the house, and she needed a complete touch up. I quoted her 5,000.00 even. She agreed but wanted it done the next day. She was wanting it done before the weekend. That was it. I came today ready to see the police. Now I am here."

Serenity made some notes. "Did you do the estimate on your own?"

"We did not go inside. The three guys were in the truck. I guess you could say they all were in ear shot."

Serenity nodded, "I need clear responses Ignacio. Did the other workers hear the estimate?"

"Yes, because we were all surprised when the lady said she would have cash. I promised to pay them in cash the same day."

"So, you are saying that the victim announced that she would have cash today for the work?"

Ignacio thought, "Yes, I guess so. We were all excited as the workload had been low lately. The guys even went out to Oyster's Pub to celebrate. I could not go as my wife made a birthday dinner for her aunt."

Serenity continued taking all the information down. "Ok, and where were you early this morning, sir?"

"I had dinner with the family last night. Relatives were in town, so we had a family breakfast. I went there directly from my house. My wife and family can vouch that I was at the house until I went to work on the dock job. I checked in with the dock master so they will have a record of when I showed up. I do know the guys were hungover. I assume they were at the bar until late, but I cannot vouch for that."

Serenity concentrated on notes. "Ok, Ignacio, do any of the guys have a record?"

Ignacio laughed. "You can't find help here without a record. I have my employee files at home. I can email them to you. I have nothing to hide. I can say that none of those guys is a killer."

Serenity finished the interview and felt comfortable sending Ignacio home. Clifton came back from the secure house. Serenity asked him to call Ignacio's wife and confirm his alibi to be detailed. She also asked Stella to pull the records on the three workers.

Jacob was nervous and jittery sitting in the Chief's office. Vito was on the phone and then went out to Stella's desk.

"Looks like they found a relative, Stella. A cousin is named Edie Regan. She lives in Ft. Lauderdale. She is going to try to get here tomorrow afternoon. The autopsy will take a while before she can get the body. The mayor is setting her up at the Sunset Resort. She emailed you the room information. We need to have someone get her from the airport tomorrow. It's going to be busy. Let's keep the coffee going. We can call in help from the Sheriff's office, if needed."

Vito came back into the office. He was an imposing figure to Jacob who was a small man and shy. Vito sat on the edge of his desk. "Ok, Jacob Schmidt, I am not going to sugar coat this. We have a dead old woman. Where were you early this morning?"

Jacob thought, "We went for drinks at the local bar. We all got wasted. I called my wife for a ride. We slept until about 5:00am. We have a newborn, and we don't sleep much. She was mad at me for having to take the baby out to pick me up. So, I promised to get up with the baby."

Jacob was the strong silent type. He had been working in construction since he was a teenager. He was born and raised on Marathon key. Like a lot of locals, his parents worked in the resorts and had a pension for drinking. He married his high school girlfriend after she was pregnant. The police station was not an unfamiliar place. However, he had never been involved in a crime so violent as murder.

Vito stared at the young man. "We will check it out with your girlfriend. Have you ever met Esther, the victim, before?"

Jacob answered quickly. "No sir, the first time I saw her was when we went with the boss man to do the estimate."

Vito paused again. "Have you ever committed a crime, son?"

"I got speeding tickets and petty theft from when I was younger. I have never done anything violent. I have been in small fights, but I don't instigate anything."

Vito walked back around his desk and sat in his chair. "What can you tell me about your coworkers?"

Jacob thought for a moment. "Elias is cool, but he can be a jerk. He had some trouble up in Miami. Ignacio is willing to take on those that need a chance. Elias left the bar before us. He said he was going to walk home. He was drunk. I would be surprised if he were out of bed before 8am. We were all kind of late this morning."

Vito nodded. "Ok, what about Lincoln? What do you know about him?"

Jacob was hesitant. "Well, to be honest he is weird. Even at the bar, he stays to himself. I know he had a rough time when we were young. His granny was mean and would whip him in front of us all. We felt bad for the kid. I know he participated in something big a few years ago. His sister bailed him out and got him a fancy lawyer. Piper is super-hot and loaded with money now."

"Ok kid, you are ok to go. Don't leave town and I don't want to hear gossip about this. That woman was a human being, and she deserves better, understand?"

Jacob nodded and ran out like he was afraid they would change their mind. Vito had their clothes and shoes photographed to show there was no blood spatter.

Vito stayed in his office to yield press phone calls and conference with the Sheriff and the Mayor. Stella went in with him to take notes. Payton was watching everyone. Elias was taken into the back room for his interview. This was the perfect chance. There was a call regarding a minor car accident. She changed it to a crash with aggression so Clifton would have to take the car and go out. She did not have much of a window.

Payton motioned for Lincoln to follow her into the storage room. She locked the door after him.

"Linc, what the hell is going on? What have you told them about your alibi? Piper texted that you were at her house this morning and were acting strange. Did you tell her anything?"

"No Payton, but I have never lied to Piper, it's killing me. She has always been loyal. This is wrong." He beseeched her with his eyes. "I think I should just tell the truth. I am tired of lying and sneaking around. Now, this murder thing. I'm going to look like a liar, Payton!"

"Shhh, keep your voice down. You need to ask for a lawyer. I will contact Piper as soon as I can. If you did not do it, you would have no worries. The problem is the mayor is now involved. They need someone to blame this on." Payton listened at the door to make sure no one else was coming.

Lincoln sighed, "Who better than the son of the Baker trash, right? They are going to love pinning this on me."

"Listen, with your violent past and no alibi, you are in deep. Say nothing and ask for a lawyer. Piper and I will take care of everything else. They are going to come to get you soon, are you ready? Linc, you can't have a nasty attitude. This new Chief is no nonsense, and he is not a local. Please, for me. Say nothing."

Lincoln grabbed her as if she were drowning. He looked into her eyes and saw fear. He could not betray her, he never could. Though he would never have her fully, he could not let go of the little time they had. He wiped her tears with his fingers and grabbed her neck hard. He kissed her with so much passion and fear that he would do whatever she wanted.

Chapter Five: Best Friends

Childhood, Piper 18 and Lincoln, 16

Piper was already married to Lachlan at this time and was working full time at the hotel. She was also newly pregnant with Rory. Lincoln was living with them, but he was having a tough time dealing with Lachlan. Lincoln had always been the beloved brother. Now, Piper is split in several directions. Soon she would also have a newborn. Lincoln was spending more time away from home.

Payton had just started community college. She was missing Piper's companionship as well. Lincoln had latched onto Payton like she was a life raft in a raging sea. At first Payton had resisted his advances. Her family expected a suitable marriage with another high standing local family. Payton thought they were such hypocrites. They had treated Piper and Lincoln as their own, but they would not welcome them as marriage partners for their upstanding clan.

They used to all meet at a certain beach after school. It was out of the way and tourists rarely traveled there due to the terrain. One hot night Payton had gone to their spot. She did not find Piper or Lincoln. She was crying and was having a challenging time in college. She just wanted to be an officer and if she did not pass her parents would insist, she just got married. She admitted that she was too weak to oppose them. She sobbed and screamed. She was sweaty from the run there. She decided to remove all her clothes and swim in the ocean. It was the only time she felt free. She swam around and underwater. It felt like heaven on earth. When she turned to start to go back to shore Lincoln was there. He reached out to her. He was not a little boy anymore. At that moment she saw the amazing and sensitive man he had become. She ran into his arms and Payton has never been with another man in that way since. She told her fiancé she wanted to wait until marriage. This was a lie as she just only wanted to make love to one man, Lincoln Baker. Now, all their lies and sneaking around was becoming a hardship. Payton did not know how it would all turn out, but she could not bear it if Lincoln was hurt. This was her lover of ten years. Now it could be a disastrous ending.

Serenity looked across at her interviewee and tried to get a read. He was calm and looked bored more than anything else. He was not sweating or jittery like the others.

"Ok, we have here, Elias DeBussey. Now we understand that you all were at the victim's house yesterday while your boss did an estimate?"

Elias yawned, "Yeah, the old lady wanted stucco work done. She was going to pay in cash so we were all excited because we could get paid right away."

Serenity asked while taking notes, "Where were you this morning before work, sir?"

Elias was abrupt with his response. "I left the bar early and walked home. I was in bed with my old lady until I left for work, at about 9am. She can verify as she is always on me about not staying out all night."

Elias continued, "Before you find out, I had some charges up in Miami. Domestics with my ex-wife. You will also see that most of those charges were dropped. She just wanted to get the kids in the divorce, but I am clean."

Payton checked the hallway and front area before exiting the storage room with Lincoln. She held his hand as long as she could. It was just in time as Vito and Serenity came out to get him for his interview. Stella went down to the other office to get the background checks. However, Clifton came back abruptly complaining about tourists and driving. Payton decided she would never have enough time for a call without looking suspicious. She hated to send it via text, but she had no choice.

TEXT to Piper from Payton

Piper, murder in town this morning. Lincoln's crew is being questioned. Get lawyer and get down here asap. No alibi, Mayor involved. I must go. Delete this text right away!

Piper heard her phone alerting, but she was in a meeting, and she never interrupted them. If she did, then the staff would think they all could be on their phones. She concluded the meeting with their goals and the staff dispersed to their areas. Piper was glad it was over, and she went to her office to check her emails. She had forgotten about her phone and completed her emails. She then checked her makeup and sat on the office sofa to check her social media. She kicked off her shoes as she had been on her feet most of the day.

TEXT to Piper from Lachlan (Honey Bug)

Hey baby, I will grab dinner, don't worry. There were lights and sirens in town all afternoon, Payton will know what happened. Anyways, Rory needs glue for his project, can you get some from work? Call me later if it is late.

TEXT to Piper (Mommy) from Rory (Baby Boy)

Ma, need glue, puhlease!!! Love ya

She smiled until she saw the text from Payton. She deleted it as she was told. She trusted Payton as much as Lincoln so if she said she would do it, she would. She did not understand why they would question Lincoln in a murder? That was absurd, he was a gentle soul. It was Piper that got in all the fights in school. Payton and she took karate together. Lincoln hated it because of the violence. She contacted her lawyer, Stuart Schockmolden. He was the best lawyer in the Florida Keys. He did every kind of law. He was a good old local lawyer and had excellent connections. He told Piper to meet him at the substation. She tried to get a hold of Lincoln, but it just went to voice mail and there was no response to texts. Piper contacted Inez, the night manager, and asked her to come in early due to a family emergency. She grabbed her things and would call Lachlan from the car. He will be on his own with the kids tonight.

It seemed like Piper was always going to police stations due to her family. The first time was with her mother Mikaela Baker. Piper was young. She was not sure how old she was, but Lincoln was just a toddler. He was a fussy baby, and Piper often would get his bottles and make sure he ate. Thomas had come home to their trailer on a drug binge. As usual a big fight started. That was when Mikaela still had her part-time job and was trying to be a fit parent. Thomas started throwing his wife around the trailer. Piper would shield her little brother with her body. A lot of the times, Agnes would call the police to get Thomas off the property. Mikaela would go to the station and file a report. However, she never followed up. In those days in a small town, it was different. The Chief or Sheriff would hold Thomas for a few days until he sobered up. He would then go back to the trailer and be the dutiful husband for a while. Once Mikaela gave up and started into the heavy drugs, it was over. Piper was getting older and wiser. She knew she was too young to fix her situation. If they did go into foster care, it was likely that they would split up. Piper would never let that happen. She would make sure there was someone there for Lincoln.

Lincoln was brought into the Chief's office and sat as Vito and Serenity spoke over papers. They excused themselves to retrieve some information. Serenity went into the other office to make calls. Vito, Payton, and Clifton met at Stella's desk. They had received background information on the workers.

Jacob Shmidt {3 speeding tickets}

{Misdemeanor theft, fine and probation, 2022}

Elias DeBussey {Domestic battery}

{Child Support Delinquency}

Lincoln Baker {battery & Aggravated Stalking}

Serenity returned. So far, the alibis for the men checkout. They just needed to finish with Lincoln. Serenity motioned to Vito to a quiet area of the station.

"Chief, this is a small town. All these guys have known each other since birth. That includes Clifton and Payton. My concern is God forbid someone is charged there may be an issue of conflict of interest somewhere. I don't see any of these kids as murderers.

I mean my son knows them and my husband coached them in little league."

Vito sighed, "Yes, it may become an issue. Right now, we have all the interviews recorded. I do think that only you and I should handle the persons of interests. Let's keep Payton and Clifton limited on the case. They should not be transporting or speaking to any suspects or handling formal questioning.

Vito and Serenity returned to the interview. They now knew about the violent past of the now person of interest.

Lincoln sat and awaited the questions. He did not agree with Payton and felt he had nothing to lose. He felt confident that there would be no evidence against him. Lincoln was sensitive when he was a child. However, as a man he developed hostility and would talk before thinking.

Vito led the interview. He gave a soda to Lincoln. "I know you have been here a while Lincoln. I assure you we will get you out soon. We just need some assistance with this one. Now, you and your boss and coworkers were at the victim's house yesterday, correct?"

Lincoln put on a brave demeanor, but he did not trust police officers since his incident years ago.

"Yes, she wanted an estimate for work and Ignacio brought us along. Then, we all went out to the local bar and got drunk. I got a ride home and went to bed."

Vito leaned back in his chair, "Ok, son, is there anyone that can confirm that you were home all night and went straight to work? Who gave you the ride, we need an alibi."

Lincoln shrugged, "No, my roommate is out of town. I was alone. I went to my sister's home for breakfast at about 9am. I will not tell you anything else. It's none of your business."

Vito nodded and moved his chair close to Lincoln. "Now, did you know that lady was paying in cash?"

Lincon nodded, "Yes, she told all of us. That's why we went out to celebrate an early payday. Usually, we must wait until the boss gets paid."

Vito leaned closer to Lincoln. "Now, you are the only one with violent crimes. You only make money in tourist season and have no alibi. What do you have to say about that?

Lincoln did not hesitate. "Everyone makes their money here during tourist season. I don't have anything to say. I did not kill some old lady. You need to look elsewhere. Why is it that the Baker family is always getting hassled by the law?

Serenity gave a note to Vito. He opened it while keeping eye contact with Lincoln. The note said that the victim of the violent charges was the mayor's son. Lincoln was still paying reparations to the family. He still owed $5,000 on the balance.

Vito glared at Lincoln. "You ever hear of a circumstantial case, son? For right now, you are being detained until we decide if there will be charges."

They all heard commotion in the main office. Vito handcuffed Lincoln to the chair and followed Serenity out. He saw Clifton and Payton arguing with a tall blonde and a gray-haired gentleman in a suit.

Piper was demanding to see her brother. "Lincoln has an attorney, and he should not even be speaking to the police. Who is in charge in this backwards place?"

Vito took charge immediately. He had whom he now knew was Lincoln's sister have a seat in the chairs with Payton. Serenity was on the phone with the county prosecutor to verify that Lincoln would be charged with first degree murder. The attorney Stuart Schockmolden was shown into the office to speak with his client.

Vito rolled up his sleeves. It had been quite a day. This blonde sister was a handful and just as hostile as her brother. She was also extremely sexy and confident. Vito could not help but notice her. He tried to focus back on the murder case.

Piper sat there as Payton went to get her a coffee. The new chief was just as intimidating as she had heard from Payton. She had to admit that the rumor about him being handsome was spot on. However, he was arrogant and would not allow her to see her brother, just the attorney. Lachlan had their accountant on standby in case they needed bail money. She could not believe this was happening again. She had just started to warm up to Payton again after that debacle. Payton came back with the coffee. She sat with Piper and glared at Clifton. He was staring at Piper with his mouth hanging open. He was an embarrassment to their department. Payton grabbed Piper's hand to calm her down. Piper was a force to be reckoned with if she loved you and her brother was her best friend.

Piper was determined but confused. "Payton, why is he here, who is this old woman?"

Payton looked toward Clifton and whispered to Piper. "Last name is Klink. An envelope of money was taken. The whole work crew knew about it. Lincoln has no solid alibi and a violent record. All the others were cleared."

Payton was upset and used the handkerchief that Vito had given her. "Of course, Lincoln is the scapegoat for this town. When will they just let my family live in peace?"

Vito was in the back office with the prosecutor and the mayor on speaker phone.

The chief was fair and did not want to put a murder charge on a young man without due cause. He did have to admit that Lincoln had a violent past and no alibi. He was one of four who knew the victim had cash on hand for the construction work. The other three have solid alibis. This left Lincoln as a person of interest. He also has the money owed to the state which would be a motive. Also, the amount needed is exactly what was stolen. The DNA results would be months away and there was no guarantee that there was anything from the killer caught.

Vito thought they should investigate further. He did not want to be rushed by political influence. However, despite the concerns of Vito and Serenity, the prosecutor wanted to charge him in the morning and press first degree murder charges.

Meanwhile, Stuart introduced himself to his client again. They already knew each other from Lincoln's previous charges.

"Well, young man, I see you are in another little predicament here. You have powerful enemies. I thought I told you to remain low key."

Lincoln took a deep breath, "I did not do anything then that he did not deserve. Also, I did not murder an old lady for a few dollars either."

Stuart waved his hand, "Nobody cares if you are guilty or not, unfortunately. They are going to come here and take you for the ride to the county. Now keep your mouth shut. You have done enough damage. It is after hours so you are going to spend the night. Watch your back and talk to no one. They will charge with a crime in the morning, so we should get bail. They are also going to do a news conference. It is already on internet feeds. Hold on because this is going to be much worse than the other charges. You are lucky Piper is your sister. There's no way you could afford me, kid."

Stuart opened the door and motioned to Vito. The chief against his judgment prepared Lincoln Baker for transit to the Monroe County Jail and courthouse for booking and arraignment with the Judge in the morning. Lincoln was searched thoroughly, and his clothes were taken. He was dressed out in gray sweats.

Pictures were taken to document if he had any injuries that may have been self-defense. His wallet, phone and watch were taken as his belongings. They asked him if he had a backpack or anything else that would have been in the work truck. Lincoln told them that he had thrown it away at the docks because it was dirty. He said Piper had given him money for a new one.

Serenity took over to drive Lincoln to the county jail. Piper was allowed to hug him, but Payton had to remain professional. There was press beginning to gather in the front, so they took him out the back.

Piper was staying strong on the outside, but she was inconsolable in her heart. Stuart assured her he would be working on this, and they should be at the courthouse in the morning. He advised her to bring her husband as well to show family ties to a good name. He let her know that they would be getting a warrant to search Lincoln's apartment and not to go there for anything until they were done.

Payton and Clifton were to get the search warrant signed at the prosecutor's office and then the county sheriff would conduct the search. Payton assured Piper she would help as much as she could.

Stella was staffing the information line as the press was calling non-stop. Piper sat down for a minute as Stuart left to get his work started. Vito gave her a fresh handkerchief and sat with her. Piper was grateful but thought it was old fashioned to have cloth handkerchiefs. This guy really was not one of the locals. He just sat with her until she calmed down a bit.

"Mrs. Campbell, I want you to know that I am not done investigating this case. I plan to be as thorough as possible. You have fearsome enemies in this county. Off the record, your brother is being railroaded. I know that your lawyer would advise against it, but I would like to hear from you."

Piper was surprised that he seemed genuine. She really felt that this tough guy from New York wanted to help. She knew she should not talk to the police, but she knew that Lachlan would not understand as he blamed Lincoln for everything. She needed someone in her corner.

"I may regret this, but I want you to know the full story. I don't know why but it really matters to you what happens to my brother." She made sure Stella was out of ear shot. "Can we meet in Key Largo? There is a restaurant on a boat that is quiet and private. They are discreet and we should not be recognized." He put his number in her phone. "I will call you when I can get away. Thank you, Chief."

He held her hand. "It's Vito, I hope to hear from you soon." Vito watched as Piper drove away. He had a feeling that he was going to be in trouble. It was the start of a bad film noir movie.

Chapter Six: Arraignment and Enemies

Mayor Alicia Travers stared in the mirror of the bathroom at the Monroe County Courthouse. How she handles this homicide was crucial to her political future. She had her eye on the state government, and her family could not afford any hiccups. Payton entered the restroom to try to get a break from the family. She was dismayed to see the mayor in there as well.

"Well, Payton I am glad to see you give your support to the family. I know Declan appreciates your presence. Your uniform looks great. Also, we will be announcing your official wedding date next week. I would appreciate it if you would answer Declan's texts. This will be a busy time for our families. You're such a pretty girl. I hope you have enough sense to comprehend what this marriage will mean for you. It's time to grow up and make adult friends. The Bakers have always been in trouble. If you take my advice, you will leave them behind and look to your future. Declan is my only child, and he wants you. Don't make the wrong decision. Now, let's go out and make nice with the reporters, dear."

Payton should have spoken up at that moment. She should have stood tall against Alicia. She could not bring herself to talk against either family. Her future was determined for her since she was born. If only, she had not met a shy, sensitive boy named Lincoln.

The county building community room was packed with police and reporters. Vito and Serenity had a presence, but they knew politics well. The Sheriff and Mayor were running this and had all the power. Vito took note that all the gang were there. Alicia had her husband by her side. Bryan looked perfectly groomed in an expensive suit that complemented his wife's dress. Declan was the consummate male athlete and would never go against his parents. Declan was their golden boy and there was nothing his mother would not do for her son. Vito was not sure how Payton got wrapped up with this family. It could be because her parents were important landowners in the area. Declan was certainly a prize physically, but the personality was lacking. Vito had to keep it professional but his instinct as a long-time officer told him that young Mr. Baker was innocent.

Piper and Lachlan waited for the press conference to begin. They were ready with bail money as soon as the amount was available. Stuart sat with them as the arraignment was scheduled soon after the press release. Piper was terribly upset but managed to maintain her perfect demeanor. She had learned early on never to show weakness, and she now had a lot of enemies here. Lachlan had always supported Piper no matter what. He had not yet gotten a chance to sit down and speak with Piper. It seemed that whenever they were about to live happily ever after her brother tried to destroy it. Lachlan used to see Lincoln as a surrogate son, but his love had turned to frustration. Piper had vowed her love and life to him but deep down both knew that Lincoln would always be her priority.

Monroe County Sheriff Michael Hanover was ready to begin the press conference. The mayor and her family, including Payton, stood behind him with other Sheriff officers. "Thank you all for coming. It is to my detriment to announce that there has been a homicide in Marathon. The victim was 80-year-old Esther Klink. Her family is obviously devastated and are making their way into town today. We are sad to report that we do have one of our locals in custody, Lincoln Baker. He will be arraigned in a few hours on official charges of first-degree murder. Now, the mayor would like to address her town."

"Thank you, Sheriff Hanover. The mayor's office is pleased with the work of the Marathon police and the Monroe County Sheriff's office. Now, we are early in this process. We can tell you that my office will make sure the Sheriff and police have everything they need. We can depend on our prosecutors to build a detailed and solid case. Marathon and Monroe County take pride in their low criminal activity. We take offense to this dangerous criminal harming one of our elderly and beloved residents. America comes here to vacation and relax. It is our desire to keep this area safe and tourist friendly."

The Sheriff came back on and let them know that they would not be taking any questions as the investigation was early and the arraignment pending.

Lincoln sat alone in his cell. His lawyer advised that he would be charged this morning and hopefully out with bail as soon as possible. He did not want to put Piper through all this. However, he could not stop thinking about Payton. She needed his strength. He could not let her marry Declan Travers and become a zombie trophy wife. They had dreamed of running away together where nobody knew their identities. He had suffered for her before, and he would protect her again. Piper was his family and had taken care of him all his life. He was a man now and needed to face conflicts on his own. Payton was his future. He did not want to live in the past anymore. Piper thought she was over their childhood, but she was still a victim. She had everything they had ever dreamed of yet there was a part of her that would always be the little girl with the addicted parents.

Prosecutor Virginia Newton awaited the arrival of the judge and the defendant from jail. She had never had an arraignment so crowded in this small town. She did not know a lot about this defendant, but the mayor was pushing this case hard. This poor kid had some dangerous enemies. However, she had always been known for her calm demeanor and her ability to be fair. She was not going to be rushed by the political machine. She would work with the evidence and investigation. They still needed an autopsy completed but her boss made it clear that they would not be waiting for that or the lab testing.

Lincoln was brought in through the side door and sat next to his attorney. He turned and Piper was with Lachlan in the first row. Payton would not look in his direction. She was sitting with Declan and his parents. Lincoln saw that she looked sad and stressed. Even with all he was facing, he wanted to go and hold her. He could not stand to see her hurt. The Judge entered and read the charges for the defendant. First degree murder was all that Lincoln heard. This time he had a real chance of doing hard time. Lincoln entered a plea of not guilty. The prosecutor asked for him to be held without bail. Lincoln knew this meant he could sit awaiting trial for up to a year.

Stuart argued that the case was circumstantial, and Lincoln had no money or passport and was not a flight risk. He was born and raised in the Keys and knows no one out of the area. He would be with the Campbells. They are an upstanding family from the area. He had already planned a motion to dismiss based on lack of evidence. The judge indicated that due to the seriousness of the crime bail would be set at 1 million dollars. He scheduled a date for new motions for next month. Stuart advised Piper that Lincoln can be bailed out asap. It will still take hours as he will have to be processed out of jail.

Piper and Lachlan ignored the mayor and her family. She spotted Vito in the room. They locked eyes and Piper turned right away and grabbed her husband's hand. They went to a local café to get coffee. Luckily, the reporters did not follow as they were awaiting the mayor. They sat in silence at first. Lachlan reached for her hand.

"Piper, you must communicate with me. You know what happened last time. It nearly tore us apart. I think we should have my parents pick up the kids for a little bit. They don't need to be exposed to all this trauma. We also must continue to work. This bail has taken a lot of our savings. I do not want to have to touch the kid's college fund. I know how close you are to Lincoln, but that kid is a walking problem. When are you going to let him be a man?"

Piper kept her composure, "Lachlan, I am not going to go over this again. When we married, I told you that Lincoln and I were a package deal. I am the only one that ever took care of him. I am not going to abandon him now. Go ahead and arrange for the children to stay with your parents. We need to stay in town to be seen and make a united front for Lincoln." Her phone chimed and she received a text from Payton. She wants to meet me. Piper ignored it for now. She had to focus on getting Lincoln out.

"I will support you as I always have, honey. I am scared to lose you. This is a strenuous situation. You know how you are, babe. You are going to let the case consume you."

"Lachlan, what am I supposed to do? Please, I cannot oversee all this and worry about us as well. Can you just give me some slack on this? We are so close to making an offer on the hotel and being financially secure for life. I promise, I can handle it. You can put the kids to bed early and join me in the hot tub. I think we can both use a drink, too." Piper leaned over and kissed her husband. She wiped the lipstick off his lips and smiled. He was a great guy, and she knew she was lucky. She hoped that they could survive this crisis.

Lachlan received the text from Stuart that they could come down to the county building and pick up Lincoln. They hurried to the building and met Stuart at the county jail section. He warned that Lincoln was not to leave the town of Marathon. He was released to be at Piper's home only and must sleep there at night. He must attend all court dates. Stuart would file the first motion to dismiss based on lack of evidence. It was standard and they were not to count on that. Lincoln was not to contact any of the victim's family. Stuart would be visiting soon to interview and start to prepare a defense.

    Piper waited anxiously for Lincoln. He appeared from the exit door and Piper hugged him right away and led him through the reporters and on lookers to her jeep. Lachlan drove and they did not speak during the drive. As they got to Lincon's apartment, they went in to get his clothing. His roommates were not there and there was evidence tape of the forensics team's remnants were left. Lincoln went to his bedroom to pack a bag. The apartment looked the same as the last time Piper was there to clean. She could not imagine what the police would be looking for here. She knew Lincoln was not a killer. He did not have that kind of instinct. This whole thing was ridiculous to her. Lincoln finished and they continued onto Piper's home. Piper did notice that he used a duffel bag. She guessed he did get rid of the backpack as she instructed.

Chapter Seven: Out on Bail

Lincoln was visiting with the children as Piper made up the guest room. She freshened the sheets and unpacked his things. She also stocked the mini fridge with snacks and sodas. Lincoln had been obsessed with Twizzlers since he was little. She finished and sat on the bed and cried. She always wanted Lincoln to stay in this room. She even painted it blue, his favorite color. She just wished he were here under different circumstances. She imagined what he would have become if they had grown up in a family like this or home like this one.

Lachlan watched from the door and waited. There was his beautiful wife. They had exchanged vows and gave each other their bodies, but there was a deep part of her that he could not touch. She would have been furious if she knew Lachlan was watching her in a vulnerable moment. Piper rarely broke down in front of anyone. This trial may be the breaking point for his young wife. She was not even connecting with the children. It would be easy to hate Lincoln if her was a jerk or on drugs like his parents. Lachlan felt eternal guilt that he just wanted his brother-in-law to disappear or get his own family. Lachlan's marriage was on a collision course.

They all ate dinner that night and tried to ignore the 'elephant in the room.' Piper was still getting texts from Payton and ignoring them. Lincoln sat in silence unless he was speaking to one of the children. Vito also sent a response to a text she sent earlier. They were going to meet in Key Largo tomorrow afternoon. Piper knew that Vito thought Lincoln was innocent. She wanted him on her side, and she rarely met a man she could not persuade.

Piper made sure everyone at the table had what they needed. She had given the nanny and housekeeper the day off so it would just be family.

Piper wanted to address everyone, "Children, Uncle Lincoln is going to be staying with us for a while. Now your father is going to drive you to your grandparents' tomorrow. If you hear anything negative about Lincoln, it is not true. If you need to talk to me or dad, you can call us anytime."

The children all nodded. They were unlikely to question their mother. They finished their meal, and Piper sent them to the playroom. She poured wine for the adults.

"I think we could all use this today. Lincoln, I know you don't want to hear this, but you must follow the bail rules. You must stay here and check in weekly with the bail agent. If they call or show up, you must be available. I know it will be boring for you, but Lachlan has a garage and shed full of sports equipment and tools. You can use anything you want."

"Piper, I appreciate you and the bail money. I am not a child. I understand how serious this is, but I am innocent. How can they have evidence if I didn't do it."

"Sweetie, we know you are innocent. Lachlan and I will support you no matter what. I just do not want you lying around here or trying to see Payton and get in more trouble. We have various enemies in this town that would love to see us fall. We must stay united as a family now more than ever. I know you have issues following rules. I'm only going to say this once because you understand how much we love you. We are on the line for a million dollars. This is before the lawyer fees. Not to mention the clients Lachlan may lose from his business. If we do not come out on top, we may be destroyed financially and crush whatever good reputation the Campbells have built in this town." Piper stood and stretched. "Of course, I don't have to say to remain clear of Payton and any of her family. Did y'all see her standing with the Travers family as if they were already married? Once Payton is married you can drop your childish crush and focus on building a career."

"Da** it, Piper. Would you leave Payton out of it? She did not do anything either. She is trying to help us. It is hard because she is a cop. She cannot officially support a murder suspect. You always judge everything she does negatively. Are you jealous of her because she had a family that loved her?"

Lachlan stood up, "No way, Lincoln. Your sister has sacrificed everything for you. You will not speak to her like that in this house."

Lincoln stood up as well. "I am not a teenager anymore. She is my sister, and I am responsible for my relationship with her. You have no idea where we came from. You never lived in a trailer with no electricity or water. We only had each other." Lincoln excused himself to Piper and went to his room.

Lachlan sat down and Piper grabbed his hand. "Honey, it's ok. He is scared and that is how it comes out. Imagine if you were charged with the worst crime there is, and you did not do it."

Payton sat in her ocean front condominium as Declan was making breakfast. He had insisted on coming over that morning. He said he could not listen to his parents anymore about the murder case. Payton was perturbed that Piper would not answer her texts. She had to find a way to see Lincoln.

Declan served breakfast and coffee. Sometimes she wondered if he was gay. He readily agreed to no sex until marriage. He also had a profound sense of style and good hair. She was quite cold towards him. He was just trying to make his parents happy. They did have that in common. Mothers that were overbearing and scary. She sat looking at him and sipping her coffee. He was quite an attractive man. She wished she could just love him. It would make life so much easier.

"Babe, now that Baker kid will be out of our lives for good. We can announce the wedding date and start the planning. Mother thinks we should use the Rose Room at the country club as it is on the ocean. They can open the large sliding doors so it will be an outside ceremony."

Payton felt nauseous. "You don't think it is morbid to announce a wedding while there is a murder case in the news. Linc is one of the locals. Don't you feel any loyalty?"

Declan was shocked, "Honey, how can you say that after he tried to kill me?

Payton rolled her eyes, "Is that how it happened? As I recall you and your goons cornered him, and he won the fight."

Declan was angry now. "He followed us to the club and tried to get me out of the way. I should have known by the way he looked at you. As if he had a chance."

Payton finished eating and grabbed her gun belt. "I must go into work. There is a lot of paperwork. I'll see you tonight."

Declan kissed her and held her hands. "I cannot wait until you get rid of this cop thing and just work in real estate."

"Honey, I love being a cop. It makes me feel like I have a purpose."

Declan scowled, "You will have a purpose, babe. You will be making grandchildren for the mayor. Now be a good girl and take your lunch. I made sushi, so put it in the fridge when you get there." He then grabbed her butt and went to clean the dishes. Payton was so confused.

Payton could hardly stand to be in the same room as her fiancé now. He was aesthetically perfect, but he would do whatever his mother said. He used to be a fun and sensitive guy. They would travel and do every water sport available. The problem was she could not stop wanting Lincoln. It seemed as if no one wanted Payton and Lincoln together. Payton's parents adored Declan and could not wait to join the two wealthy families. Piper had no idea that they were in love or meeting in secret. Piper always thought she was the beauty pageant winner and Payton just another local. Lincoln was to do whatever Piper wanted and Payton hated that. Lincoln was trying to save enough money to propose to Payton. However, once he was found guilty of the incident with Declan, he owed money in court fines and restitution.

Payton parked her SUV down the street from the Campbell home. Lachlan left with the children early. Piper left soon after, of course looking perfect. Payton waited until she saw the housekeeper leave for errands and walked to the house. She went through the back sliding door. She checked all the rooms and did not find Lincoln. She went out back again and saw him sitting on the dock. He looked so tan and beautiful. She still got butterflies when she knew he was around. Payton looked first to make sure no one else was around in that area. She walked down the dock and sat next to Lincoln. He immediately took her hand, like he felt her presence. She leaned on his shoulder, and they sat that way for a while. They did not need to speak as they knew the circumstances were out of their control this time. Payton could not convince the mayor and her family to help this time. Lincoln would not hurt Payton by revealing their affair. It was so complicated for these two people to love. Payton had to get to the substation. Lincoln walked her to the side of the house. They kissed until they were out of breath. Lincoln held her tight and whispered in her ear that everything would be all right. Payton felt safe and protected when he held her like that. He then watched her as she walked down the block. He closed his eyes until he could not smell her perfume any longer.

Piper was exhausted but Lachlan was right that they had to keep working. The bail money was a large hit for them to take financially. She did her usual rounds and then hid away in her office. She was about to leave to meet with Vito. She wanted to get information. He was a good ally to have, and she could sense that he was attracted to her. She had to use her looks before to get out of trouble. She would do anything to support her brother. She had taken his beatings from Agnes when they were young. He was so fragile then and she would not let him suffer from grandmother's hand. She checked her makeup and made sure her cleavage was highlighted in her uniform. She let down her long hair and was ready.

Everyone was refreshed and back at the substation in the morning. Vito had sent Clifton early to pick up the victim's family in Key West. They were still awaiting the autopsy report, but the prosecutor was going to make sure it was sent to them and the Sheriff upon completion. The small bit of DNA was at the state lab and that would take a while even with the mayor's influence. Vito had Serenity and Payton go back to the neighborhood and do old-fashioned questioning of neighbors and businesses. They were also to check for any surveillance on nearby homes and buildings. Poor Stella was screening the calls from the press and the 'clingers. Those were the people that gave false information to try to be involved in large cases. Vito signed the pertinent reports. When Stella seemed stable and was ok to be alone, he slipped out.

Vito took his own pick-up to Key Largo to see Piper. It would have been better if he were not seen as the Chief of Police. Especially being seen with the family of a murder suspect. He was not sure why he was taking this risk. It could be that he felt that the kid was innocent and framed. It could be that he could not stop thinking about Mrs. Campbell. She was not only gorgeous but intelligent and driven. He rarely met women that could match his intensity. He stopped home to change out of his uniform. He chose jeans and a dark blue polo shirt. He combed his dark hair, completing his tan and handsome look.

Payton reached the restaurant first and asked for a private table off to the side. She sipped on sweet tea and waited for Vito. She felt a hand on her shoulder, and she turned to see Vito. He was in regular clothes and looked tan and virile. She stood and shook his hand. She motioned for him to have a seat. He did notice her shirt buttons revealing her tan cleavage. He was a gentleman and dared not to stare. She was worth more than someone leering at her. He ordered a lemonade and waited for her to speak.

"Vito, if I can take that liberty, sir. I am the closest person on this earth to my brother, Lincoln. We grew up as a team and endured abuse and neglect from our parents and our guardian, Agnes. Lincoln would not have killed this woman. Especially for cash. Lincoln knew that if he were in real trouble, that my husband and I would provide anything. Also, feel free to call me Piper."

"Ok, Piper, I am not the one that needs to be convinced. I am sure your attorney will tell you the details of how to combat the circumstantial evidence. Also, they don't really need a motive to convict, but it helps with a jury. I am hoping with some more investigation that we can find inconsistencies. There are other men with sold alibis. Make sure your attorney gets an investigator to dig into those. I can only discover new evidence or find more information. I cannot go back to the witnesses unless there is a reason. Otherwise, I will appear as if I am impartial and could lose my job, do you understand?"

Tears welled in her eyes. Vito reached for her hand and rubbed it softly. "Piper, I promise if your brother is innocent, I will find a way to fight them legally. I already have the officers in the neighborhood questioning and looking for cameras. We will find something. Is there anything you can tell me that might help?" He then wiped a tear that rolled down her cheek. He thought she was still mesmerizing even when crying. He had to be careful with this one.

"Well, we don't know what his alibi is right now. He's been quiet with us. I am hoping he reveals it with his attorney. You can try the bar where they were as I am sure they have cameras. There are a lot of fights and violence. I would send Clifton if I were you as since you are from out of town, the locals may be reluctant to talk."

"I have only been the chief here for a brief time. Tell me, how did a woman so young get the solid business reputation you have in town?"

Piper blushed, "It was not easy, Vito. I had to overcome poverty and family addiction, violence and so much more. I was determined to change the next generation. I will make sure my kids have the best of everything. I think when you must work for something so hard, it drives you to achieve even more. Most think Lachlan is the big shot. I bought the construction company and made him President. I hope I am not bragging but I am quite capable of taking care of myself."

She flipped her hair up as it was hot and then sipped her tea. "The reason I need your help is that the families like the Travers want nothing better than to bring down a Baker. I need allies on my side. I felt like you would understand me. Did you grow up in New York?"

Vito leaned in more. "Oh, so you have been doing your research on me. Either that or you have been talking to Payton. I was born and raised in Brooklyn. I had a single mother who worked two jobs to keep us off the streets. My father left when I was a baby. Anyways, my mother taught me to be able to hustle in any situation. I worked my way through college and got hired onto the NYPD. I needed a slower pace of life, so when no one wanted the transfer, I took it. Now that I am sitting here with you, I have made the perfect choice. I also have a daughter. She is my top priority, but I am not against adding a woman to my life and in my bed. It gets lonely on these warm evenings."

Piper looked down. She wanted to avoid his deep brown eyes. She felt like he was seeing through her. "Vito, I can feel you are fond of me, but I am happily married."

He turned her hand and looked at the large diamond. "Yes, the ring is extraordinary. I am not trying to disrespect your family. I would not do anything to hurt you. I just want a chance to make you happy. I see in your heart that you need support, and you are not getting it at home. Think about what you want. I will still help you regardless of our relationship status. Piper, I will not wait. If you tell me no at our next meeting, that is fine. If you do not give me an answer and show up, we are going to my house. Do you understand?" Piper was taken aback as no one ever spoke to her that way. She nodded that she understood.

"Ok, we will do that then. I need you to stay in touch in case I need more information for the case. Piper, stay strong. He is lucky to have you on his side." Vito realized they were still holding hands. He suggested they should leave as it was getting late. Vito walked her to her car, and she gave him a hug that caught him off guard. He was a bit taken aback by the proximity. She smelled of flowers, and he squeezed back feeling the arch of her back. She jumped in the car and smiled. Vito watched her as she drove away. He hoped he was not making the biggest mistake of his career.

Payton did not know how she was holding up. She was trying to deal with her fiancée and his family. Lincoln was facing life in prison or the death penalty. Now, she was out in the heat of the day knocking on doors. So far, no one saw anything, but she had many complaints about tourists. Payton finished the block and saw Clifton speaking to the last resident on the list. She hoped that he had better luck.

"Hey Clifton, nothing down here. How did we do by the beach access?" Payton fanned herself with her notebook.

"Yea, I got a Mr. Crawford at 879 Beach Road. He says he was waiting for the medical van for his doctor's visit. Well, he is looking out his window and sees a guy in a hoodie headed towards the beach." Clifton flipped through his notes. "Did you know we had a medical van for seniors? I wonder if they will go down to Key West. My aunt has this balance thing…"

Payton was getting frustrated. "Clifton, get back to the witness, please."

Clifton replied. "Sorry, yes, he said he only saw him from the back. It was a dark colored hoodie. White male medium build. Oh, and he was carrying something. The old guy said It could be a backpack or like a duffel, dark color. He has a ring bell but does not know how to use it. I am sending the tech over to retrieve it. We can get a better description."

Payton motioned for him to come back to the patrol car. "It is time to see if the bar had its cameras working that night. You know the owner personally, right.?"

Clifton threw her the keys and jumped into the passenger side. "Yes, he is a good guy. Retired from Miami with the wife and bought the bar. It can get rough. Just the locals solving problems mostly."

Payton and Clifton went into the dive bar as police this time, not locals. There are certain places in the town that are unofficial local hangouts. In a resort town, the hotel workers and yearlong residents want a place to congregate without the hassle of the tourists. It is often a bar with cheap liquor and loose rules.

James Reyes and his wife Liz ran the bar for their retirement. James was often out deep-sea fishing during the morning and then bartending the rest of the day. His wife Liz was the main bartender the evening of the homicide. Liz advised that they were getting loud but that the dock workers were rowdy. She did say that there was an incident over television. There was a football game and the workers wanted to watch, but others wanted the music louder. Other than that, it was a typical night of drinking. She was not sure about where they went after. She did notice that Elias was very drunk.

"We cut him off and took his keys. He wandered out on foot, which was not unusual. Most of the men lived in walking distance from the bar." Liz could not tell them who left when of the others as it was a busy night. They did have a camera fixed on the parking lot. They would release a copy to the Sheriff's office technician.

Piper was trying to concentrate on work. She just could not be herself at this time. She had tried her whole life to make sure Lincoln was happy and successful. He fought her at every turn. Payton had kept texting her, so she finally agreed to meet tomorrow. They were best friends growing up until Lachlan came into the picture. Piper was working hard and had to also run a household. It caused Payton and Lincoln to become closer. Piper did not like this at all. She knew the family would never accept Lincoln as a son-in-law. Her brother would only be hurt. Piper thought that it had been resolved until Lincoln ended up in jail. Declan had accused him of stalking him and assault. It was exactly what Piper was afraid would happen. Payton was a wonderful person, but she could not stand up to her overbearing parents. Lincoln deserved a nice young woman who would appreciate the sensitive and intelligent man he is.

Back then, Piper had to pay for a good lawyer again. Lachlan was not thrilled about going into their savings. However, he knew that Lincoln would always be her number one priority. It had put a strain on their young marriage. Piper knew that Lincoln did not pick a fight with Declan. Why would he challenge three men to a fight. Payton had been there and knew the truth. However, Lincoln did not want her to testify. He took a plea deal to protect Payton. Piper was furious because it could have affected his diving license. He was lucky to find Ignacio, who was willing to take a chance on him. Now, this was a disaster. She knew that Lincoln did not kill that woman. He was his own worst enemy. He was also covering something up again. Piper would not let this happen again. She would do anything to protect her brother.

Piper had been texting back and forth with Chief Vito since their meeting. She used an app that would delete the text chain on both ends after 24 hours. She needed an ally on her side that was within the police or government. The mayor was very well connected, and they were up against a formidable opponent. She had already spoken with Stuart to get their investigators on the other workers' alibis to make sure they are solid. She was awaiting the video from the bar to see if there was anything there. She had laid good groundwork and was positive that Vito would give her any information. She was hoping to get his attention, but she would go farther, if needed. He was exceptionally good looking. She was happy with her husband, but this was business, not pleasure.

Vito was back in uniform and at the office. Stella was assisting the technology forensics team with the ring bell and video from the bar. Clifton and Payton were writing up their reports on the neighbor and the bar owner. Vito returned to his office to look over the case file. He was hoping to find something that would help Piper. He felt that it was right as he had interviewed Lincoln himself, and he did not think he was lying. He had to admit that he did have a personal interest in the beautiful Mrs. Campbell. She seemed vulnerable and needed a man to understand her and support her. As far as he had seen, the husband was not very attentive. He wanted to be the person that she needed. Since his ex-wife he had not been so attracted to a woman.

Stella knocked and came in with the videos. Serenity followed and sat down.

Serenity had her notebook, "Hey chief, so the cousin of the deceased is safely in town and at the hotel. She is having dinner with the mayor tonight. They are awaiting the autopsy results and then they can release the body to her chosen funeral home.

Vito nodded and motioned for her to continue. "Ok, the ring camera from the witness is not particularly useful. It shows a white male with medium build walking towards the beach access. He has a hoodie covering him. Unfortunately, all the men involved wear a hoodie. The bar tape confirms that Ignacio was not there late, but the other workers were present.

Vito sighed, "It does not help either side. Let's get a copy to the prosecutor and they can delegate as needed. What else have you got?"

Serenity looked over her notes, "Yes, Elias was cut off by the bar tender and was in a foul mood. He was the first to leave and they took his keys and cut him off. Now, the tape confirms that he was the first to leave and he walks off toward the beach. I know what you are thinking but the beach cams are broken and due to be replaced later in the week. Jacob is seen getting into an older model Toyota with a woman and a car seat in back. Now, Lincoln is staggering. He walks down the block, and a car picks him up. We cannot see the license or the type of car."

Vito was surprised. "He is lying. What is it with this kid? If he has an alibi, why would he not tell us?"

Serenity leaned forward, "The lawyer and him are planning to use it. Now it will be out there so if I were them, I would name the person. What could be worse than being accused of murder? Or is it an illicit affair? He was dating the mayor, what do you think?"

Vito almost spit out his coffee, "Really, Serenity. I think you may be right about him protecting someone. The mayor detests the Baker family, so I doubt that. There is a person that does not want to be revealed."

Piper waited at the dockside bar for Payton to show up. She was terribly busy, but Payton was insistent that they needed to meet. She ordered both drinks and checked her phone. Vito texted her to meet later that week to compare any new information. Payton walked in and Piper waved her over to the table.

"Piper, thank you so much for meeting me. I know you are busy with everything going on with Lincoln. I really wanted to see if you needed anything. You know I really miss the bond we had previously. I thought you could use a friend."

"Payton, I have trusted few people in my life. Most have let me down or used me for their personal gain. I have had to hustle and scrape out a life for Lincoln and me. When I found out you were messing with Linc's head, I was furious. You know that your family would never accept him as a son-in-law. Lincoln is sensitive and he loves hard. He was obsessed with you. Just when I thought he was doing better, this sh** happened. You told me before that your affair with Lincoln had ended. This is true, correct?

Payton took a drink and was nervous, "Yes, of course. I barely see Lincoln anymore. Not since I helped with his scuba license. Piper, this world does not fit into your perfect framework. Lincoln and I did not plan to fall for each other. It was organic and we were both lonely. Loneliness can be an aphrodisiac in a small town like ours. My family is complicated and there are consequences if I do not fall in line with them."

Piper listened quietly, "If you love him and you want to help me, please get him to tell his alibi. Also, speak to Declan's family and tell them to call off this witch hunt."

Payton's eyes welled up with tears. "I was not born with your fortitude Piper. That is why we were good friends. I was sensitive and you were technical and utter perfection. Beautiful and intelligent. Your fortitude is amazing. We were yin and yang together. I cannot control Lincoln. As much as you think Lincoln is emotional and flighty, he is not. He is stubborn and no one can make him do anything. I wanted to tell you in person that Declan and I have set a wedding date for next year. The mayor is announcing it soon. I did not want you and Lincoln to find out from the paper."

Piper shook her head. "Payton, a little advice. Do not go through with this wedding. I know your spirit, and you would be miserable. I always told you. Stop letting life happen to you. You must start creating your own narrative. Are you giving up the Police force?"

Payton hesitated. "Declan would like to start a family right away. He thinks the job is too dangerous for a mother."

Piper placed money on the table and gathered her purse. "I will always be your friend, Payton, but I cannot deal with this now. I must save my brother's life." She took Payton's hand. "I will always be your biggest champion. I do not forget how kind you were to us as children."

Chapter Eight: 7 months later

Attorney Stuart Schockmolden sat in his law office in the conference room. His assistant Melissa showed Lincoln and Piper to their seats.

"Ok, all. We are coming up to our trial date within a few weeks. We have exhausted all motions, and it looks like the prosecutor is still going ahead. It does not look like there will be a plea offer, but they still have time."

"Lincoln, I am going to ask again, are you going to name your alibi?" Lincoln shook his head.

"Ok, kid, I am going to keep asking as you are aware you can get a life sentence or death, correct?"

Lincoln was quiet as usual. "No, we will have to think of something else."

Stuart was not surprised by the response, "Ok, let's move on then. Now, our biggest evidence is that Elias' girlfriend has recanted her alibi. She had left him and claims he bullied her into saying that he was home that night. She now says she never saw him until he came home at a quarter to nine and showered for work. The best part is he takes his clothes with him and does not leave them in the laundry. This is our reasonable doubt and the other suspect. Now, he was cut off by the bartender and is in a rotten mood. Upon further questioning, the bartender says that he had money on the game that night. She overheard that he lost and that is why he was drinking heavily. So, this guy needs money and now has no alibi. Now, the Mayor has pull to keep the case going. However, we are coming back strong."

"Now Elias has an ex-wife that may also be a good witness or at least give us more information about him. We are going to speak with her tomorrow and see what she knows."

Piper was feeling good about their defense. "Stuart, what about the autopsy and any forensics?"

Stuart looked through the file on his laptop. "Good Question, Mrs. Campbell. The cause of death was suffocation by strangulation and manner of death is homicide. There was no DNA located. The substance under her fingernails was inconclusive. None of the men had scratches on their body. This is going to be a straight circumstantial case. Now, they can win but we have a strong defense. We never know how a jury is going to decide. Also, they do not need a motive to convict. It is to our betterment that they do not have a motive. Lincoln could have gone to family if he needed money."

Stuart stood and looked out the window for a minute. "The mayor has announced her running for re-election. With this big wedding she is merging with two of the wealthiest families in the Keys. It will be a coup if the prosecutor gets a guilty verdict. Welcome to politics, young people. There is not always a fairy tale ending. Sometimes it is a Grimms fairy tale."

Piper and Lincoln headed for her Jeep and drove home. They were both on edge as the trial grew closer. They had settled into a routine the best they could. The children were back home and in school. They were having trouble with the other children because their uncle was on the news as an accused murderer. The press had died down, but it would start again the closer they get to trial. Piper was visibly upset about Lincoln's lack of alibi. She suspected it had something to do with Payton. She did not want to believe it as it would mean that two of the most important people in her life were deceiving her.

Piper was the best at making outside appearances perfect. Lachlan and she appeared together as a unified front at all the hearings for motions. They even appeared on a local podcast to speak on Lincoln's behalf. Stuart was present to make sure they did not say anything that could damage the case.

Lachlan loved and supported his wife. However, she would not open to him fully. He felt her slipping away. He had a feeling it was not just the trial. She was emotionally distant, and Lachlan was afraid this was too much for her. Lincoln was like a virus that caused their family to become emotionally ill.

"Linc, even you cannot be this stubborn. Tell me the truth, are you protecting Payton?"

"Piper, no. You do not understand. You blame Payton for everything. For once, let me be my own man and make my decisions."

Piper was livid. "This is your life, Lincoln. Prison for about thirty years. Is a woman worth that? What kind of woman would ask you to do that?"

Lincoln was quiet and remained looking out the window. "Piper, I realize you have made many sacrifices for me. I love you. Let me be my own man. You are my sister, not my mother."

"I wish I were your mother. I never would have neglected you and left you in a skanky trailer for an old bitty to raise. We deserve a break. We have been beaten and degraded. I will be damned if you spend your life in prison. I built our name up from nothing. Being a Baker meant drugs and bad decisions. Now, we are Campbells, and you have a chance."

"Piper, do you think I did it? What if I did? Would it ruin your fake façade of the perfect family? Sometimes I wonder if you do this all for me or for you?"

Piper was aghast, "What, how can you say that? I am on your side. I have risked my job and my marriage for you."

Piper pulled off to the side of the road on a beach parking lane. She could not see the road for her tears. She had never asked Lincoln if he killed that woman. She had never asked because she knew him better than anyone. He could not harm anyone. He was able to defend himself and had the usual 'Baker temper.' Especially a woman. They had old school ideals and an elderly woman wound never be harmed. No matter the motive.

Lincoln thought against going to comfort his sister. She did not like to be seen as having any weakness. She had been hiding emotions from him since they were children. She was like a skyscraper. A modern, equipped landmark that was gorgeous on the outside and prepared for any need on the inside. She was intelligent and loyal. However, even the best built tower must sway at the top to keep from breaking in strong winds. He did feel responsible. He had become an incendiary to the women he loved.

Lincoln was tired of feeling guilty. Piper had shielded him in childhood. Agnes spared him from her worst moods and temper. That could have been because he was younger and did not talk as much as Piper. He was not sure. Now, as an adult he had followed his heart and pursued the woman he loved, Payton. He watched how Piper landed the man of her dreams and it was positive. However, his love for Payton caused tension and conflict.

They remained silent for the rest of the drive. They pulled up and Lincoln jumped out. Piper drove off. He watched and felt bad for his sister. However, she had never had real love. She never had anyone to love her as a child. She never learned to bond. Lincoln had Piper in his corner, but she had no one. Lachlan could never reach her inner pain. Piper loved her husband and children, but she would not allow herself to be loved.

Piper ran her fingers slowly over the shoulder and back muscles of a sleeping Vito. This was the place she had been most comfortable in these months before trial. It was a small house painted yellow. The inside was a tacky teal color. The small bedroom was quiet and had an ocean breeze. They would lay nude under a crisp white sheet that smelled of lilacs. Piper would close her eyes and listen to the seagulls and the slow steady breathing of the police chief. She had been here with Vito at least twice a week since their second meeting. They had gone back to his place for their second meeting. Piper was the aggressor. She needed to relive stress at first. Then she found herself craving his comfort. Now, she could not wait to spend the afternoons in the small house. It was cozy and made her feel like she was on a vacation. Piper had not planned to let her guard down. She just wanted the police to be at her side. However, Vito turned out to be an incredible man. He grew up in a tough area of Brooklyn. Piper thought that he was a gentleman and cared for women because of being raised by a single mother. He made her laugh, and it had been a while since she had just had fun. They also spoke of parenting and their love of family and loyalty.

Vito awoke and stretched in bed. He turned so he was facing Piper. He pulled her in close. "I want you to move in with me. Forget that large house. It is cold and stale. I want to wake up next to you every day."

Piper laughed, "What about my kids, where will they sleep?"

"They can have the second bedroom, and I will make the porch into a room. I would build you a house from scratch."

"Vito, come on. We talked about this, and it cannot be more than it is now. I am married and we have plans. Also, I am responsible for my three children. I will not abandon them like my parents did."

"You are not leaving your children. You are leaving your loveless marriage. We will get Lincoln out and then he can come to our wedding."

Piper was uncomfortable. "We will see. I must see the children. Also, I had a hard conversation with Lincoln. I feel bad. He must be so scared. Thank you for getting Elias' girlfriend to tell the truth. I think with the ex-wife, if she cooperates, we will have reasonable doubt."

"Absolutely, the prosecutor wants us to bring Elias back in this afternoon and question him again. There is nothing the mayor can do about that. I would do anything for you, Piper. The sooner you get that; the sooner we can make a life together."

Vito could not shake off the conversation with Piper. He could still smell her perfume. He did not view her as a small affair. She was the most confident and strong woman he had ever met. She should not have struggled anymore. They could have a marriage based on love and mutual respect. They had both gotten into young unions for the wrong reasons. Vito did not care about her family background. She needed someone that was not a local from this island. They seemed friendly but beneath the surface there was judgment and corruption. He was ready to be a stepfather. He would help her get custody and they could live anywhere. Along with his daughter, they could create a loving family. He was ready to fight for Piper.

As Vito was lost in his thoughts, he pulled into a reserved space at the back of the police unit. A man was pacing back and forth in the alley. Vito parked the car and removed his sunglasses. He squinted and realized it was Lachlan. This was not how Vito wanted to start his morning. Especially since he had just proposed to the man's wife. He grabbed his bag and gun. He took a deep breath and approached Lachlan. He was not sure if he knew about the cuckold relationship with Piper.

"Good morning, sir. This is the back entrance. I am sure if you go around to the front desk, we can help you."

Lachlan stood to the side with a perplexed look on his face. Vito, a trained police officer in high tension situations was not prepared for this. His instinct was to keep calm and not assume that this was about Piper. It may be connected to Lincoln's case.

Vito was looking for the keys. He now did something completely out of his training. He took his eyes off a possible hostile opponent. Vito felt the familiar jarring pain of a bare fist against his jaw. He had been in enough fights as a child in Brooklyn to know the sensation of a sucker punch. Vito was a substantial male who was in excellent physical shape and trained. It took him by surprise, but it did not shake his balance.

Lachlan, on the other hand was also a large man but not a fighter. He had broken up fights between the construction workers. However, he was getting older and developed a 'father pouch.'

Vito dropped his bag and subdued Lachlan with two solid jabs to the stomach. As Lachlan slumped over in pain, Vito restrained his arms. He could smell the alcohol coming off his opponent. He was not angry but had a sort of sympathy for the man. Piper was an amazing woman, and he must have known that she was in love with someone else.

Clifton and Serenity then burst from the back door. Clifton pulled his firearm, and Serenity got her handcuffs to restrain Lachlan so he would not resist.

Clifton returned his weapon to his holster. "What is going on back here, chief? This guy attacked you. Is he nuts or drunk? Hey, isn't this that rich guy whose married to the hot blonde? I'll take him in and start the paperwork." Clifton reached for Lachlan.

Vito motioned for him to back down. "It is ok, we are not filing charges. Serenity, you can go back to work, thank you. Clifton, get these cuffs off him. He is not a danger at this point. Can you get an ice pack and coffee, please? Also, let us keep this out of the rumor mill, please?

Lachlan stirred and immediately reached for his bruised stomach. He had to get his bearings. He remembered drinking at his office. He had liquid courage and decided to confront Piper about everything. He wanted to talk about finances, family, and their future. She had been at the office more than usual and he knew there was a strain somewhere.

He drove down Ocean Avenue and saw Piper's Jeep at a small house on the beach. He pulled in at the dock across and watched. Soon, he did see Piper emerge in her work uniform. She opened her door and threw her purse on the passenger side. She then stretched and stood looking at the ocean. Lachlan was about to get out and approach his wife. Suddenly a male exited the home. He was a tall, tan male with dark hair. Lachlan had seen him before but could not place his face. Lachlan was queasy as the man grabbed his wife and kissed her for several minutes. They looked at each other as if they could see nothing else. Piper drove off as the man walked back to the house. Lachlan then saw the police cruiser. Now he knew why the man was familiar. It was the police chief. He should have known there was something odd about all the visits to the station and her constant late nights.

Lachlan felt that he did everything for Piper and the only thing he wanted in return was her unconditional love. He knew that she would never leave Lincoln or let him become an independent man. However, he would never have thought she lacked passion and love from their marriage. With all the financial planning and political aspirations, they had lost that intimacy they first had before the mansion and the children. Piper was so vulnerable now with the trial looming ahead. This son of a bi*** had taken advantage of her one weakness. He promised that he could get Lincoln released. He waited until the Chief left and followed him. Lachlan did not remember anything after that.

      His head felt like it was five hundred pounds and he used his elbow to push himself up without aggravating his rib area. He was in an office. He saw a gun case with rifles and handguns visible through the glass. Chief Vito was at his desk on the phone. There was a steaming cup of coffee in front of him. Lachlan sipped the coffee and placed a large ice bag on his side. There was noise from the small squad room outside. However, the shades were drawn, and no one could see him.

Vito ended his call. "Do not worry man, no one will know that you were here. I am Vito Ramone, the new police chief."

Lachlan coughed and sat up straighter. "F*** you, Vito. I know what you are."

Vito leaned back in his chair. "Look, I cannot blame you for wanting to hurt me. I have been seeing Piper for some months now. We are in love. This is not just a fling. I want to take care of her, and I would never hurt or devalue that woman."

Lachlan rubbed his head, "If you are trying to make me not want to hit you, it's not working right."

Vito sighed, "You did give me quite the hit if it makes you feel better. I will let that one go because she is your wife and I disrespected your marriage. If you do it again, I will make it so every appendage on your body will ache and bleed."

Lachlan was furious but had no doubt that the Chief could in fact cause severe harm. He stood up to stretch but found out that he was still buzzed.

"Look, chief. I am a businessman. I do not go around getting in bar fights or following my wife to men's homes. That was on instinct, but I won't apologize for defending my marriage. We took vows and they broke. However, they were destroyed far before she was in your bed. She was never mine completely. Lincoln will always be her top priority. Then the kids and on a good day me. Her work, I am ashamed to say, may also be above me. She must be perfect to the outside world and the community. She does not realize she is amazing already. The mansion, boats, and money mean nothing to me. I was a means to an end. Fighting you was the right thing to do. If I did not want to fight you, what does that mean? Am I not a real man? Or do I know we are already inevitably damaged as a couple? Regardless, we have children. I need to speak with her, and it needs to be handled in the family. If you love her as you say, give her time. She has never trusted anyone else than Lincoln. She is a hard addiction to end."

Vito had Clifton take Lachlan out the back and drive him home. Serenity drove his car back home and parked it. Vito did not want to do anything to hurt Piper. He knew that she would be his soon. He had to have patience.

Payton stood in her childhood bedroom with her mother. She stared at her reflection in her wedding dress. It was breathtaking and it was what she always dreamed of as a child. Except the groom was Lincoln and not Declan. Her mother took a picture.

"Honey, you look like a sad but lovely bride. You are wearing a designer gown and will unite with one of the most powerful families in the Keys. Are you still thinking about the Baker boy? Now, I love him as well, but he cannot do anything for you. He is also likely to spend the next 30 years in prison; you want to be a prison wife?"

"Mother, why did you marry Dad? I mean I never see you hold hands or kiss."

"Payton do not be vile. The young people today with all their kissing in public. Marriage is a contract like anything else. I had many boyfriends when I was young. However, your father had a good education and was stable. Don't you think I also wanted excitement and adventure? You had fun, now it is time to marry Declan and get pregnant. Now, take the dress off before your siblings' spill something on it."

Payton used her phone and sent the dress picture to Lincoln. She wanted to go to their spot and jump in the ocean. The closer the trial and wedding got, Payton was more confused. She was brought up to obey her parents and be agreeable. Her affair with Lincoln was her only time in life to do something just because it was desirable.

Piper returned home looking for Lincoln. She found Lachlan alone. The children were out with the nanny and Lincoln was out on the boat. Piper changed and went to her home office to look over bills. They had another payment to the lawyer, and she had to balance the money. Lachlan appeared at the door.

"Piper, we need to talk. I think now is good as we are rarely alone nowadays." Lachlan sat on the chair opposite her desk.

"Lachlan now is not good. I have so much to do, and the kids will be home soon. It has been so stressful, and the trial is coming up. After Lincoln is acquitted, we can go on vacation."

"Right, it is always in the future. What if he is convicted? How are you going to manage that? You must think about every possibility."

"No, I refuse to think that way. I have always thought positively about everything. I will not accept it. He will be let out. I was thinking he should just stay here. He can save his money for the diving business. He will also be getting his trust soon. He does not even know that he will be able to start over."

Lachlan, frustrated, went around the desk, and shut her computer. He took her hands and led her over to the sofa. "Piper, you are not hearing me and that is the problem. You are colder than ever now. I am not sure what is going on, but I cannot do this anymore. You shrink away from me when I touch you. We do not talk anymore unless it is about children. This is not what we wanted when we said our vows." His eyes welled with new tears.

Piper was taken aback as Lachlan was not one to show his emotions. She took a deep breath. "Lachlan, what are you really trying to say?"

He left the room and came back a few minutes later with an envelope. "Piper, I want a divorce. I will stand by you for every court date with your brother. I still care about you, and I want him to have the best defense. Once this trial is over, I would like you to move out and sign these papers. You will find that the business assets are split evenly between us.

Before she could speak Lachlan continued, "I know that you like everything orderly, but we are not a contract. I would prefer to have primary custody of the children. I would never keep them from you, but I think they would do better to stay in this house with me. Also, if there is the slightest chance you would contest the divorce or custody, I will have to act. He handed her another envelope. I had a long talk with your sexy lawman. In here are pictures from a private investigator. I particularly like the one on the not so secluded beach. I don't think I am that flexible. It is a New York thing."

Piper flashed with anger. She ripped both envelopes from his hands. "I was just a teenager when we met, and you promised me the world. I love you and you gave me the most beautiful children ever. I needed to be secure, and you represented that security. I don't think I am in love with you. I'm a woman now and I was a child when we wed. I deserve to have a chance to be a soul mate and so do you."

Piper began sobbing and Lachlan held her. She felt sorrow for the children. They decided to tell them together after the trial. They would have joint custody, and Lachlan would stay in the house. Piper would buy a house within a few miles, so the children would have them both close by, Piper did not feel it was the right time to introduce Vito to her family. She had to focus now but she was looking forward to starting a life with him. He was exciting, fun, and loyal. This will be her time for her happiness. She just had to get Lincoln out of trouble.

Marvin Heath was the investigator for Stuart assigned to question the ex-wife of Lincoln's coworker, Elias. She was in Miami and did not seem to have a high opinion of her ex-husband. Marvin pulled up to the small home in a middle-class section of Miami. It was mostly working people and families. There were iron screen doors and fences, so it was a bit of a higher crime area. Marvin was from Connecticut, so he was always intrigued by the houses. Even the poorest neighborhood had palm trees and humidity. Not much different from wealthy except for crime. All the houses were pink stucco in this neighborhood. It reminded Marvin of an older song. He played the song and listened a bit before approaching the interview.

Marvin rang the bell and heard children and a small dog inside. A woman answered the door but kept the screen door locked. She was a younger woman but looked as though she had a hard life.

She shushed the dog and looked at the man, "Can I help you sir, if you are selling something, my deadbeat baby's daddy left us destitute."

Marvin laughed, "No mam'n, not selling anything at all. I am from Marathon, and my firm is defending a young man for murder. Now, we think your ex may have information. Would you be willing to answer some questions?"

She thought for a moment and then unlocked the door and motioned for him to enter. There were two children running around and a small dog. He moved some toys and sat at the kitchen table.

Marvin took out his notebook and prepared to take notes. "So, you are Elizabeth DeBussey, correct?"

She nodded, "Yes, everyone calls me Beth for short. Can I get you some water or coffee?"

Marvin answered, "Yes, water would be perfect. I am going to just get into the details. How was Elias as a husband?"

Beth fidgeted with the toys on the table. "He was plain mean. It was mostly when he was drinking but he always had a short fuse. Now, if you caught him on a good day, he was super friendly and gentle. If he were in a bad mood, it would do you best to leave him alone. He used to push me around when I was pregnant too."

"How about finances, was he a good provider?"

"No way, he never could keep a job for a few months. Then he got into gambling. It started innocent with doing sports pools at the local bar. Then, he got involved with some scary people in the underworld of sports betting. I was terrified as these guys would come to the house looking for him."

"Did you ever call the police?"

Beth laughed, "Yes, at first, I called all the time. They never did anything until he broke my finger. That was the one that got him the charges. He left for Marathon soon after. I have been in and out of court for child support. He just moves to hide from the courts. They just started to deduct the funds from his checks. He will relocate and quit that job soon. If I were you, I would keep an eye on him."

Marvin knew their victim had a broken finger. "Beth, which finger did he break?"

She showed him a crooked and deformed ring finger. "I told him I was going to pawn my wedding ring. He broke my finger in a struggle to get it away from me. I did not have the money to get it treated properly. Now I have a permanent reminder of that bastard. Is there anything else you need to know? I need to start dinner for these kids."

Marvin closed his notebook and finished the water. "No mam'n, you have been very helpful."

Marvin turned, "Oh, one more thing, would you be willing to testify in court, if needed?

Beth sighed. "I do not want to think he could kill someone. You know he was not so bad until the gambling. I want to teach our children to be honest and good people. So, I would be willing to tell the truth in court."

Lincoln sat in the guest room at Piper's house and checked his phone. There was a picture of Payton in a wedding dress. She was breathtaking and looked incredibly sad. Lincoln was angry with everyone. He was mad at Piper for trying to keep them apart and reigning over his life. He was furious with Declan and his family for using Payton as a vessel to give them proper grandchildren. He did not blame Payton. Her family had her terrified of being disowned for being with a poor construction worker. He knew Payton relied on the security and closeness of family. That is why Piper and he were always around them when they were young. It was the family structure that they never had. At least if he were in prison, he could be free of everyone in Marathon.

In Marathon, he would always be haunted by their last name and their parents' struggle. Their mother had died of an overdose years ago. Agnes had a funeral and acted the part of a grieving mother. Piper and Lincoln knew that Agnes had abused their mother too as a child. She must have had some kind of policy on their mother as they had never seen Agnes so happy. Their father was still alive and serving a long sentence for attempted murder in connection with a drug robbery. Now, Lincoln being in jail had proven the locals correct. They always said that he would end up just like his father. Piper tried so hard, but she could not fight fate.

Lincoln knew that Piper went through life ready to fight. She had to fight her grandmother. Then she had to fight off the boys in high school. The other girls hated her because she was naturally beautiful and smart. The boys were desperate to get her alone for dates. Lincoln always thought that Piper had rushed into marriage with Lachlan. He was a nice safe place to land for her. She was so young and had worked several jobs at a delicate age. Lachlan had married her as a child. She was now a woman, and Lincoln knew she felt trapped in her marriage. He was hoping that Piper would let herself be free. Of course, the children would be devastated if their family were torn apart. Ultimately, Piper would need to make the decision on her own. Lincoln knew she never did anything without great planning and forethought.

Chapter Nine: Trial Day is Coming

Vito and Serenity had coffee and were ready to do a follow-up interview with Elias Debussey. His girlfriend, who was now an ex had changed her statement to the investigator for the defense. Serenity had picked him up at the bar. He was not happy as he had not had a drink yet. He had just got there after work when Serenity asked him to come in.

Elias was not happy this time. "What do you want now? Did that bit** girlfriend of mine say I hit her again? She is a liar. She claims she is pregnant now, too. I am still dealing with my baby mama in Miami about money.

Serenity started, "Thank you for coming in voluntarily, Elias. Do you remember the night before that sweet older woman was murdered?"

Elias nodded, "Yea, Lincoln killed her is what I heard. Took all that money too. They say that sister made him do it to pay her back. What do you want for me?"

Serenity read from the file, "I see here that your alibi was confirmed by your current girlfriend. Now see since you broke up, she is telling the truth. You were not with her the whole night and had a window of opportunity to kill the victim."

Elias crossed his arms and did not speak.

"We also have word that you are a gambler and not a good one either, did you need money? Did the bookies threaten you and that envelope with money was too tempting? Did you strangle the life out of that poor woman? You like to beat on your girlfriends, right? You even like breaking fingers to get expensive rings, huh?"

Elias was angry now. "Look, I drink and gamble too much. I may fight with my women but that does not mean I kill old ladies. Jacob and Lincoln are broke too. I have kids and there is no way I would risk a long sentence for some money."

Elias sighed, "Look my ex-girlfriend is mad because I have been sleeping with Liz from down at the bar. Her husband is the owner. He comes over to my trailer and is knocking on the windows. My girl gets pissed and starts throwing stuff at me. She moved out and now she is trying to get me in trouble. I'm a cheater, but I ain't no old lady killer."

Serenity took the lead and badgered Elias for a while more. He did not break. They did not have enough to arrest. It was another strong suspect. They would send the transcripts to the prosecutor to share with the defense.

Mayor Alicia Travers was in her office with Walter and her husband, Bryan. They were busy preparing for her next election. However, the case against Lincoln Baker was weakening every day. There were rumors that the Judge may dismiss the charges due to lack of evidence.

Alicia was nervous and paced the floor in her office as she spoke. "How did this happen? He has motive and a criminal record. He cannot even account for the time of the murder. Everyone knows he did it. The Bakers are known for violence in this town. I want that kid convicted and shipped off before the wedding and the election."

Walter was always on his phone or tablet. He looked up. "Alicia, you cannot convict without solid evidence. The autopsy was inconclusive for DNA at best. The crime scene shows nothing. Just because he grew up poor doesn't mean he is a killer. Also, the other suspect DeBussey did not appear to be investigated thoroughly. It was not such a clever idea to push the police."

Alicia was perturbed and finally sat in her chair. "If they did not finish their investigation than it is the police's fault. If this blows up, we put all the blame on that new chief. He is from up North, the locals will have no reason to trust him."

Bryan stood up and got a drink. "Alicia, you need to calm down. Now, we put ourselves in the investigation. Let's make sure it gets finished. What if there was more evidence that came out. We can get him to confess. Wait, isn't he obsessed with Payton? She can get him to confess. He doesn't appear to be that bright. Men like that run on emotion, not book smarts."

"You would know, darling. Please leave the politics to us and have another drink."

Bryan adjusted his tie and sat down begrudgingly.

Walter was disturbed, "I don't think we should interfere any longer."

Alicia interrupted, "No, I like where this is going. What if he went to see Payton that night and he left angry and rejected and went towards the murder house. He needs money for someone like Payton, right? He thinks the money from the old woman would get him a start in life. What do you think?

Bryan was skeptical, "How are you going to get Payton to go along with this?"

Alicia smiled, "Payton is nothing if not chronically obedient. That is why she is the perfect daughter-in-law. It is time she started paying her dues for this family."

Payton was in her condominium with her mother and her future mother-in-law, mayor Alicia Travers.

"You want me to do what?" Payton was appalled at her mother especially for suggesting she turn on Lincoln.

"Honey, calm down. Just see if you can get him to confess. It will be better for everyone. If that does not work, you just testify that he was with you and you rejected him because of his lack of money. Then, he leaves angry towards the murder house."

Alicia added, "Listen to your mother, dear. If he confesses, I will personally deal with the prosecutor to get him a lower sentence. We can lower the charges and get him ten years before parole. He would still be young when he gets out. Besides, his father is in prison. He would have ended up there regardless. Then we have the wedding, and I win my bid for reelection. It's a good plan."

Payton could not believe what she was hearing from them and sat down as if she were nauseous. "I have agreed to marry Declan. I have let you choose every wedding detail. I even submitted to having a baby right away. Also, I must leave the police force, which I love. Why are you doing this to me? You are taking away everything I love!"

Payton's face turned red, and she began sobbing.

To her surprise her mother stood up and slapped Payton. Even Alicia was taken aback. "Payton Christine, you stop being an ungrateful brat! Your father and I have made every opportunity available to you. Did you want to have a life like the Baker family? We kept you safe and now you are marrying the most eligible bachelor in Florida. You will speak with Lincoln and get him to confess to you. I am exhausted with this Lincoln Baker nonsense. If I had known he would be so much trouble, I would have never let him into my home as a child. We helped him and that arrogant sister of his all their childhood. Now, it ends. Do you understand?"

Payton was shaking and just nodded her head. All she wanted was to get out of that room.

Alicia was still shocked but impressed. "Well, that is settled then. Why don't we go over the seating chart while all the women are together, huh? Payton, get ice for your face and calm down. These are 'first world problems. Do you think I was in love with Bryan? Of course not, he is a moron. He was also the top real estate agent in the Florida Keys. I knew he would be successful. You had better get a backbone young lady. It is a tough world out there."

Payton made her excuses and advised that she would be having drinks with the bridesmaids. Payton had a bloody lip from the slap and got in her car to head straight to Lincoln. She was tired of being in the middle of her family and her best friends. Everyone counted her out and never expected anything but obedience. Even when she joined the police force, her family did not attend the graduation. She never felt more like herself than when she was working in her uniform. She could deal with criminals but not her own family. Now she was going to be married and would never be able to decide for herself again.

She pulled up to Piper's home, and she was glad to see that Piper and Lachlan's cars were not there. She parked down the street and went to the back door. She checked the kitchen window, and Lincoln was at the sink washing dishes. So, the housekeeper was out as well. She knocked quietly on the door. Lincoln turned and hoped it was not the press again trying to get a story on the upcoming trial. He opened the door, and it was Payton. She had an injured lip, and he could see her pretty eyes were wet with tears. The minute she saw him she collapsed into his arms. He closed the door and held her until she was calm. He had her sit and drink water. Payton told him directly what happened between her mother and the mayor. Lincoln was furious.

"I am going to jail anyways. I should go down to the mayor's office and take care of this permanently." Lincoln was pacing the room.

Payton was tired of him being hurt. "Lincoln, I am done. When I was there with those women, I suddenly realized that this was all my fault. They are using me for their ridiculous agendas. They do not love me or care about my welfare. I don't care anymore about what people think or believe is right for me. I am going to stay on the police force. I don't want to marry Declan. I can hardly stand to be in his presence. I want you, Lincoln. Since we were kids, I have only had one dream. That is to be your wife and have your children."

Lincoln thought for a while. "I have spent my life loving you. I have always wanted to be with you. I had to wait for the day you would come to me completely. Not just body, but your soul. Now, it is likely I may go to prison for life. I cannot let you be out here just waiting. You are too good of a woman for that."

Payton had a stern and serious look, "I don't care what happens at the trial. I want you to be free, but I am yours regardless of the outcome."

Payton stood from the chair and they held each other. They agreed that they would be one no matter who or what came up against them.

Vito had just left his apartment and wished he were still back there in bed with Piper. The substation was quiet as Payton had the day off to do wedding stuff. Clifton was out patrolling the hotels. Stella was finishing paperwork from the second interview with Elias DeBussey. Serenity was out on a robbery case. Vito had to go through resumes to replace Payton when she married. It was a shame as she was a good officer that would make a great investigator one day. He was surprised she was marrying into that family. They were not a friendly group and made enemies easily. Vito was not sure Payton had the natural shrewdness to survive that clan.

Vito was in his office texting with Piper when Stella knocked. Piper wanted to meet him that night. Vito closed his phone and motioned for Stella to enter.

"Chief, there is a Jacob Schmidt here and he only wants to talk to you."

"Really, ok, let's get him set up in an interview room so we can record. I will be right there."

Stella led Jacob and his young wife into the interview room. The woman had obviously been crying and looked distraught. Stella agreed to watch the baby for the couple. Vito entered and sat at the table with his notes and the case files.

"Hi, Jacob. It's nice to see you again. Who do we have with you?"

Jacob's voice quivered a bit as he spoke. "This is my wife, Julie. She wanted to be here. I am doing this for my family."

Vito was very curious. "Ok, what is it you want to tell us, son. If there is anything else, you know about the case we sure would appreciate the help. As you know, trial is a few weeks away. We are at the threshold here."

Jacob turned to look at his wife. She grabbed his arm and nodded as if to tell him it was ok to talk. "I killed that old woman."

Julie started to cry and grabbed a tissue. Vito was taken aback as if he was not expecting that. Vito thought it would be best to let him tell his story in full and then ask questions.

Vito wanted to be careful with this process. A confession was important. It was even more important to make sure he had the details and was telling the truth. Jacob lied in his first interview, so this was a slippery slope. He made sure he knew he could have a lawyer present and understood that he was giving his statement free of counsel and was not under duress.

"I have not been able to sleep. I have nightmares. I just keep seeing the body and then imagine Lincoln spending his whole life in prison. He is a good kid, really. He doesn't deserve that. Julie convinced me to come here. I don't want my daughter to grow up with a liar and murderer as a father. I must tell the truth and take my consequences. Even if it means I am away from my family." He grabbed Julie's hand and stared at the table for a while.

"We are struggling. With the rent and the baby, I just was not making enough. Julie is nursing and the baby has asthma, so she can't work. Her parents hated me so that was not an option. My folks are struggling too and have no money. I asked my grandmother, and she threw me out of her house and called me a 'loser.' That old woman who wanted the stucco done was flashing her money around. You should have seen her bragging that she used only cash and that she has extra money. I got drunk that night and spent the rest of our money on drinks. Julie picked me up and we were on our last quarter tank. Then the baby needed diapers, and the electric was off. I couldn't take it. I am supposed to be a man, and I cannot take care of my family. I told her I was going for a walk. It was like I was blacked out. I ended up at the Klink home in the early morning. She let me in right away. I asked her for the money first and she laughed at me. I then demanded the money, and she wouldn't stop screaming. I just wanted her to shut up but when I lifted my hands, she was dead. I took the money and any jewelry I could find. She had a huge diamond ring, and it was stuck so I just snapped her finger until it came off. She had so much money, and we had none. She did not need it, and no one would help. I dropped the gloves and stuff in a public can at the beach and walked home. Julie was asleep and I slipped back in. She did not even know when I got back as she is up so much with the baby. I tried to hang myself so they could at least get some money from insurance, or she could find a new husband. Julie stopped me and convinced me to come here."

Jacob had marks on his neck that matched his story about the hanging. He would have to be careful as the kid may need to be on suicide watch. Vito believed them and the details given matched the crime. He had Stella bring the baby back so he could spend time with them.

Vito stepped out and Serenity was back. He had her and Stella come to his office. He informed them about what was happening.

Serenity was shocked as well, "Well, we must contact the prosecutor. This is not as simple as letting Lincoln out and locking up Jacob. Nowadays confessions are hard to deal with. Especially when someone is already in custody. I am thinking it will be the prosecutor and judge that would make the decision."

Vito sighed, "Yes, you are probably right. This is a delicate process. Until we hear back from the prosecutor, this information does not leave this police station. We will give him a few more moments. Then,

Serenity, please get Julie and the baby home. Stella, start checking on some area services for the mom and newborn. We will hold Jacob here under suicide watch. We will also have to contact EMS to check his neck. We need to follow all rules. Believe me, the mayor is planning right now for the police to take the fall for her oversights. Take a deep breath ladies, this town is never going to be the same again.

Mayor Travers was in her office with Walter when the Sheriff contacted her. She slammed the office phone down and slammed her fists on the desk. The prosecutor's office advises that there will be a hearing on the homicide this afternoon.

"This is a disaster. We will look like fools. That Baker boy will sue the city. How could this happen? Get a hold of Payton now. We need her to testify that she was with him, but he disappeared. There was blood on his clothes?"

Walter rubbed his forehead in frustration. "No one can reach Payton. Not even Declan. You pushed her right into Lincoln's arms. Mayor, I cannot be involved in some kind of cover up. We just need to do damage control. Stand up there and support his release. Let's spin it so the Sheriff takes the blame. We should have listened to that police Chief, Vito. He made sure to be thorough. We can support the

Marathon police. It will help with the Sheriff taking the largest hit."

The mayor was seething. Walter was worried that she was too emotional to go in front of the public. "Mayor, maybe you should have your husband go to the hearing?"

Alicia sat and was in deep thought. "I will not let this happen. We have the re-election and the wedding coming up." The Baker children will ruin everything.

Chapter Ten: A Hearing

Prosecutor Newton was awaiting the hearing with most of the town. Her office was never keen on releasing anyone. Much less a murder defendant. However, the confession of Jacob Schmidt was confirmed with information from the crime scene. He knew details that they did not release to the public. The mayor was furious, but they were already beyond the point of no return. They had to release Lincoln Baker. Right after, Jacob Schmidt would be arraigned. They would ask for no bail, but even with bail the new defendant had no financial backing. They would be interested in a plea deal to get this case completed. The prosecutor gave the Monroe County Sheriff a heads up that the mayor's office intended to make them the scape goat. The prosecutor was furious that she was involved with the family issues of the mayor. She was the legal expert and should have made the investigation longer to get all the information. This whole case was rushed. Politics used to be about power and money. Now she was made to accuse an innocent man of murder so the mayor's son could marry the prettiest girl. It was ridiculous. She was happy that this might mean the mayor's opponent would win the election. Then, they could get back to fighting crime and serving the needs of the people.

  The courtroom was filled to capacity. Piper was in the front row. She was not sure what was happening. She had sent texts to Vito but there was no response. She was sure he was busy, but he always answered her, so she was concerned. He was in the back of the room speaking with the sheriff. She had sent him texts that she loved him, and they could be together now. Lachlan sat by her side as usual. They knew it helped Lincoln to have them both at all the hearings. Everyone was on edge, especially Lincoln because they did not know what this hearing was about.

  The Travers made sure to be there in full force. Alicia, Bryan, and Declan were all seated just behind the prosecutor. Alicia's face did not show her emotions; however, she looked stressed. It was noticeable that Payton was not there with them. The Sheriff and the Marathon officers took their seats at the back of the prosecutor's side. Vito read the latest text from Piper and sent back that he wanted to marry her and take care of her every need. Piper read it and relaxed right away. She hoped that Lincoln would get out and she could finally be happy.

The side door opened, and Lincoln was led in by an officer. He looked confident and had a smile on his face. He was wearing a nice suit and looked handsome. At this time, in the back, Payton slipped in and sat in the back row. She wore a short white dress with embroidered flowers lining the hem. Her brown hair was shiny and was up with beautiful ringlets around her forehead and neck. She was stunning. She had covered her injuries from the hit with makeup and felt strong and independent.

Next, the Judge came in and after everyone was seated, she started. "Ok, thank you all for coming today. I was made aware that there has been a development with this case. Before I address the prosecutor regarding this, I need to make something clear to everyone. This case is not about politics or the police. There was a woman named Esther Klink that lost her life in a violent fashion. The court only has her family's best interest to guard. When things occur like this today, it makes me furious and sad at the same time. I hold all the government entities responsible. I would like to make a mention of Chief Vito and the Marathon police. They had the foresight to make sure that everything was completed. They were not afraid to go back and make sure all boxes were checked. These are the kind of individuals and groups we need in this county. Now, madame prosecutor, please proceed with your emergency motion."

The prosecutor stood and began. "Your honor, the prosecutor moves that all charges are dropped against Lincoln Baker at this time."

The room had an audible gasp and reaction, so the Judge had to demand silence. The Judge then spoke, "This motion is granted with extreme prejudice. Mr. Baker, on behalf of the County of Marathon Florida, we regret this situation and since there has been a valid confession from a Jacob Schmidt admitting to taking the life of Esther Klink. You were a suspect and handled yourself as a gentleman and good citizen. I wish you a long and happy life here in Florida. I beseech your former boss to give you a chance to return to employment, if that is your desire."

Lincoln responded, "Thank you, your honor."

"Ok, if there is nothing else. We can come back in ten minutes for the new arraignment of Jacob Schmidt."

Mayor Alicia stood up. "Your honor, would it be ok if I addressed the defendant on behalf of the County politicians?"

The judge nodded and motioned for Mrs. Travers to approach. Alicia stood in front of Lincoln. No one knew what she would say, and they were all nervous for different reasons.

"Lincoln Baker, the first time I heard your name it was because my son, Declan advised that you were threatening him and his engagement to Payton Fisher. Then there was an assault on my son, and you hurt my child.

The Judge interrupted, "Mayor Travers, this is not the place…."

Alicia continued, "Now, you get away with the murder of an old woman in our county. Your family has been terrorizing this town since your grandparents. Now, you want to take my re-election."

Stuart stood up. "Your honor, I object. My client has been nothing but cooperative she…."

Alicia lunged at Lincoln before anyone knew what was happening. She managed to scratch his face before a deputy grabbed her. She was thin and wriggled free from the first officer. As the additional bailiff grabbed her, she was still kicking at Lincoln. It was a tight space behind the defendant's table, and all the bodies were intertwined. Piper had an instant reaction when seeing Lincoln attacked. She was an athletic and tall woman. She jumped over the railing and covered Lincoln with her body. Vito then was halfway to the scuffle. The spectators mostly ran towards the tussle creating a barrier. Suddenly a gunshot rang out. The noise bounced off the wood, benches and other barriers creating a significant boom. It caused the larger crowd to disperse, so Vito was able to get to the bodies on the ground. He saw one of the deputies grab Alicia's hand and force the gun out. The firearm skidded across the room under the Judge's podium. That same bailiff then had Alicia in an arm hold and had her against the wall. The second officer helped Piper to her feet. Vito was then right there and grabbed Piper from behind and pulled her away from Alicia. The second bailiff lifted Lincoln and checked him for any wounds as he had blood on his shirt. There were no wounds. Payton was trying to make her way to Lincoln but now there were officers coming in through all the doors.

    Vito had Piper and was holding her with her back in his stomach. He suddenly felt her body limp. Also, there was a wet substance spreading on his police uniform. He laid her on her side on the ground. There was a hole in her back. Vito was in shock and did not realize that Piper was shot until Payton screamed. Vito pulled himself together and the bailiff laid her on her back and started CPR. The Sheriff and other officers kept the crowd back and got Alicia in handcuffs and back to the cell doors.

    Lincoln realized what was happening and saw Piper being worked on, but blood was running from her mouth. Lachlan was on his knees sobbing. Payton appeared and helped Lincoln to his feet. They would not let him get close to Piper as they were doing first aid. They continued with compressions as they awaited the EMS. The courtroom was clear of everyone but the first responders and Piper's family. When the paramedics arrived, it was clear that Piper was gone. They called it and stopped CPR. Vito was devastated but made sure that Lincoln was able to have a moment with his sister. He knew that her brother was incredibly special, and she spoke of him all the time. Lincoln held Piper in his arms and rocked her like a child. He kept saying "Thank you" repeatedly. Payton placed her hand on his shoulder, and they held each other. Lachlan was inconsolable. He walked with the body as they took it out to the ambulance. He asked that they not use a body bag just yet. Vito held back to make room for the family to grieve. However, that night alone in the bed where he made love to Piper, he thrashed around. He was angry and intensely sad at the same time. They had been so close to ecstasy. Now he was stuck in this town with constant reminders of the woman he loved.

    The funeral was a sad event for the town. Piper was so young and vital to the small community. She was an organized person, so she had specific instructions ready in case of her early demise. She was to be cremated, and her ashes spread at the small beach area where Lincoln, Payton, and her went as children and teens. The policy paid off the house so Lachlan and the children could remain in their home. Each child had a college fund. She left letters for Lincoln and Payton separately. She asked that they be opened at their beach spot after her ashes were spread in the ocean and sand.

    The town would not be the same after this incident. There was an acting Mayor immediately and Walter was fired. Alicia Travers pled guilty to aggravated assault and was sentenced to 20 years. Her husband, Bryan and Declan moved to California and worked in real estate. The Marathon police were awarded for their investigations, and a new building was being built with state-of-the-art facilities. Vito had a tough time with Piper being gone. He could not show his grief because of the affair. He watched over Lincoln without him knowing. He knew that Piper would want Lincoln to have a good life. Jacob Schmidt pled guilty to second degree murder and was given twenty years to life. An anonymous source paid for his lawyer, and they got him eligible for parole and dismissed the death penalty.

    The memorial service was of course beautiful. Piper had laid out specific instructions for everything. She had music to be played. It was an open invitation to speak. Her co-workers and Lachlan spoke about her beauty and intelligence. After the service, only invited family members gathered at the small beach.

Payton and Lincoln stood aside on the beach as Lachlan and the children spread the ashes. Lincoln felt that the children needed that closure. Payton held his hand tight. They had not told anyone, but both their left ring fingers had beautiful diamonds. They had done a private ceremony at the courthouse. They did not feel it was appropriate to get married at a large service so close to the memorial service. Lincoln did not want to wait. He had lost his sister, and he wanted to start his life with Payton asap. He realized how short life was and wished he had married Payton years ago.

Once Lincoln and Payton were alone, they read their letters as husband and wife. They planned to stay in Marathon. Payton would remain with the police. Lincoln wanted to open his own diving school. They also wanted to help with Piper's children as much as possible. They sat in the sand and read their letters.

Dear Payton:

I knew since our first meeting as kids that you and Lincoln had a special connection. I did everything I could to prevent you from falling in love. I was afraid that Lincoln would never be accepted by your family. I have spent my whole life protecting my brother. You are my best friend. So, I hope you understand how scared I was for you to be with

Lincoln. I hope I can one day accept you both. Please watch over my children and make sure Lachlan is ok. If you are reading this, then I died young. Thank you for the best memories from our childhood. I still find peace by going to our special spot.

Your friend,

Piper Baker Campbell

To My Darling Brother Lincoln:

We were the only family we could count on in this world. I tried to shelter you from the worst of their actions. Agnes grew up with horrible abuse and neglect herself. This made her cold and unapproachable. Our mother grew up with this abusive woman and became dependent on drug use. I wanted to break the cycle of abuse. I made sure you had the best of what I could give you. Please watch over my children and make sure they use all their advantages in life. Please know that you were always my priority. Lachlan is a good man, but he could never accept that you came first in my life. Try to be his friend as he will need someone on his side. I already know that Payton will be ok because I see the way you look at her. She is a lucky woman to have your love. I tried so hard to not be a product of our environment. I hope I have not smothered you. I tried to give a perfect vision of my life to outsiders. I lived for the life I wanted, and I achieved it. I am not sure I will *ever not be that little girl in the small trailer worrying about what will happen tomorrow.*

Childhood: Piper 12, Lincoln, 10, & Payton, 11

Agnes was in a particularly foul mood that day. Piper made sure Lincoln had lunch and they then fled the house. They found a small stretch of beach. It was empty, probably because of the terrain being mostly rocks. They sat among the rocks catching small sea animals and talking. After a few minutes, a young girl came up to them. Her name was Payton. She said she had a big family, but she wanted to get away from all the chaos for a while. Before long, they were all inseparable. They met at the rocks every day. When they were due home all three would hold hands and walk along the seashore.

Now as spouses, Lincoln and Payton walked along the shore after honoring Piper. Now just the two holding hands and remembering those special days.

The End

Please leave your review on Amazon.

Author's Website: www.jwnovels.com

Made in the USA
Coppell, TX
08 February 2026